## Mighty Mighty MONSTERS

# THE ABOMINABLE Snow Kid

STONE ARCH BOOKS
a capstone imprint

Mighty Mighty Monsters are published by
Stone Arch Books, A Capstone Imprint
1710 Roe Crest Drive
North Mankato, Minnesota 56003
www.capstonepub.com

Library of Congress Cataloging-in-
Publication Data

ISBN: 978-1-4342-3892-4 (library binding)
ISBN: 978-1-4342-4227-3 (paperback)
ISBN: 978-1-4342-4650-9 (eBook)

Summary: Winter has pounced on
Transylmania in full force. While the kids
are thrilled to have a snow day, their good
times are cut short when they realize the
cause: An Abominable Snow Kid has moved
to Transylmania, and she has brought Old
Man Winter along with her!

Printed in the United States of America in
North Mankato, Minnesota.
062017
010608R

Mighty Mighty MONSTERS

# THE ABOMINABLE Snow Kid

created by
**Sean O'Reilly**

illustrated by
**Arcana Studio**

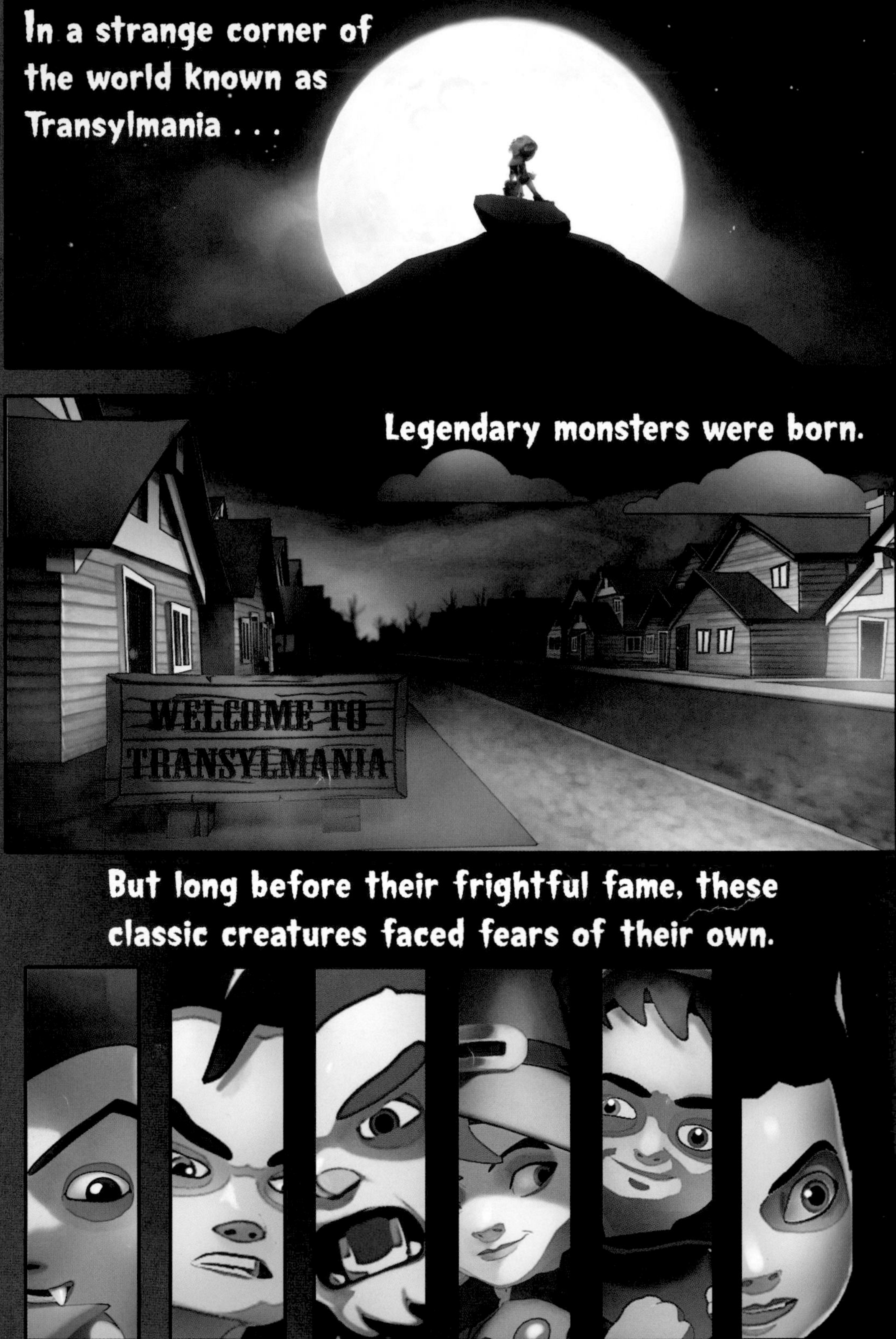
In a strange corner of the world known as Transylmania . . .
Legendary monsters were born.
WELCOME TO TRANSYLMANIA
But long before their frightful fame, these classic creatures faced fears of their own.

To take on terrifying teachers and homework horrors,
they formed the most fearsome friendship on Earth . . .

# Mighty Mighty MONSTERS

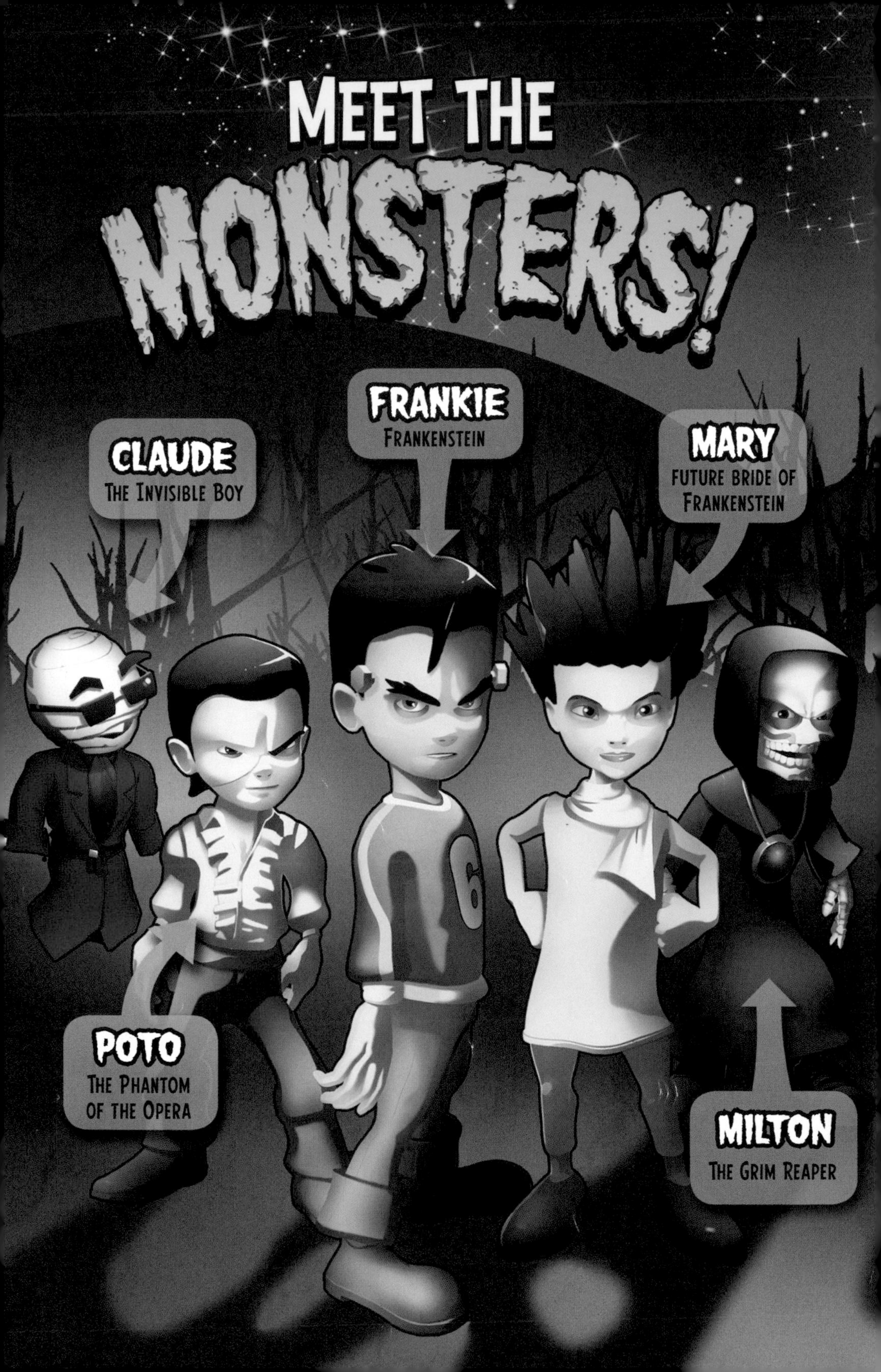
MEET THE
MONSTERS!
FRANKIE
FRANKENSTEIN
CLAUDE
THE INVISIBLE BOY
MARY
FUTURE BRIDE OF FRANKENSTEIN
POTO
THE PHANTOM OF THE OPERA
MILTON
THE GRIM REAPER

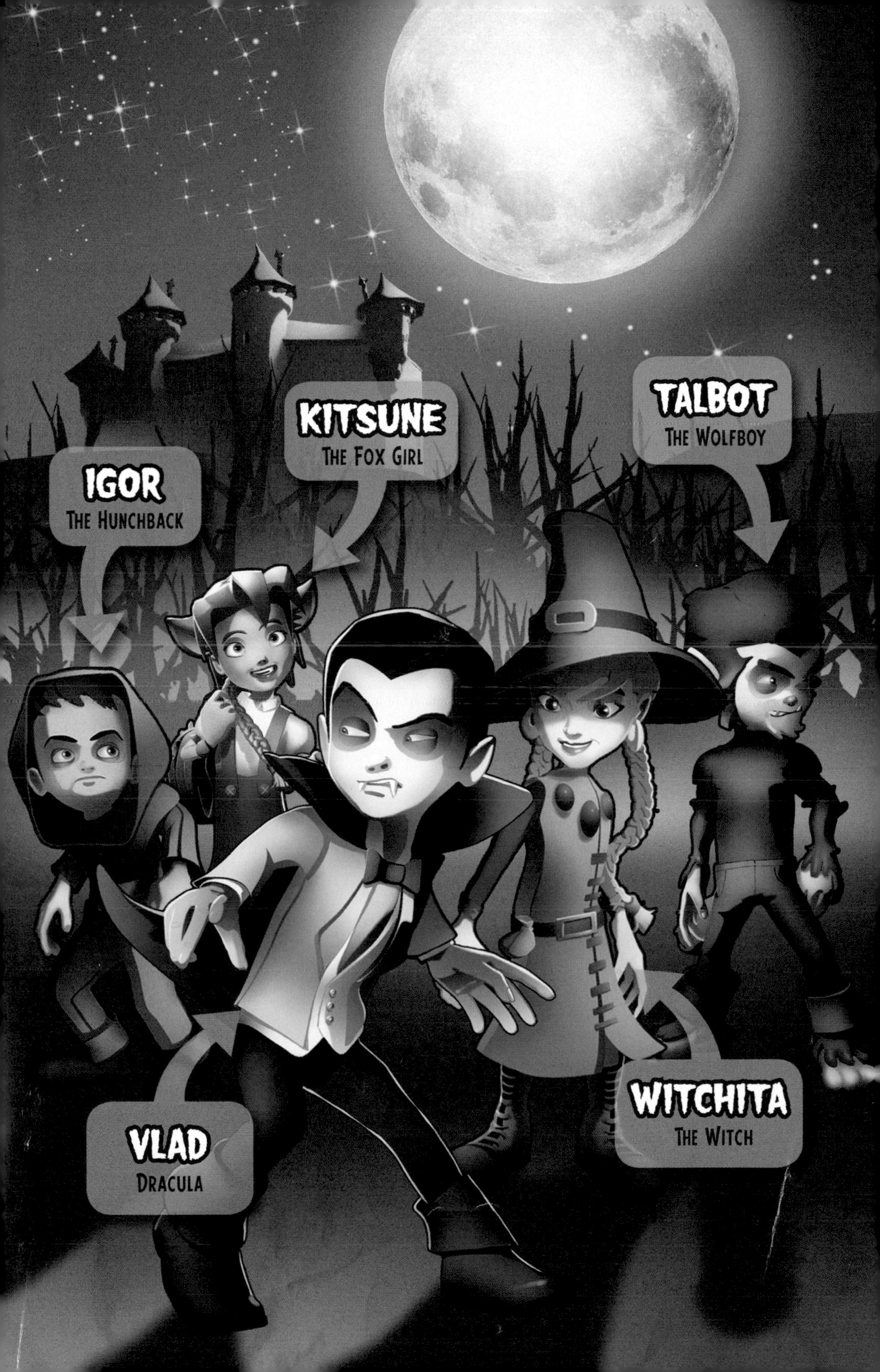
IGOR
THE HUNCHBACK
KITSUNE
THE FOX GIRL
TALBOT
THE WOLFBOY
VLAD
DRACULA
WITCHITA
THE WITCH

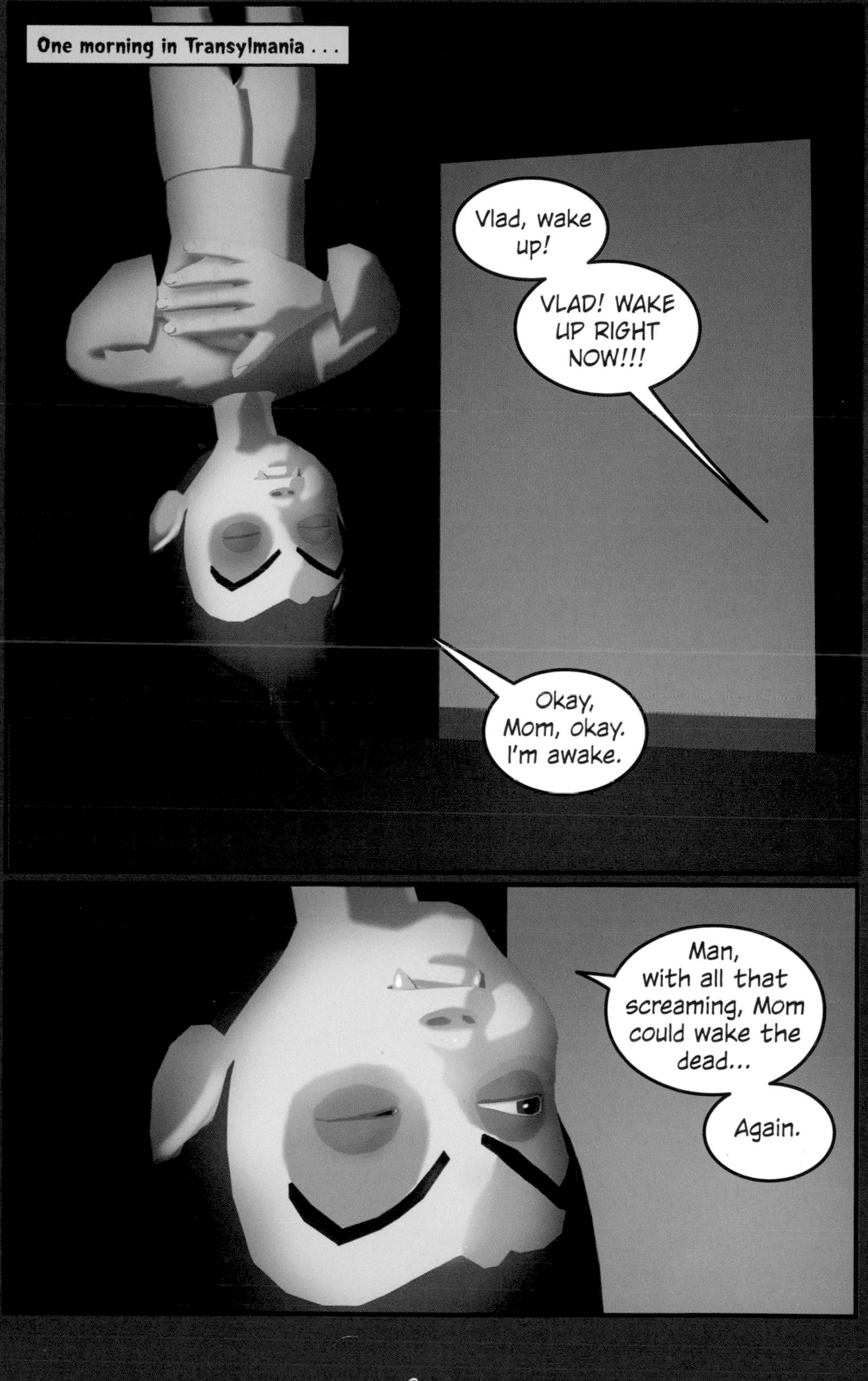
One morning in Transylmania . . .
Vlad, wake up!
VLAD! WAKE UP RIGHT NOW!!!
Okay, Mom, okay. I'm awake.
Man, with all that screaming, Mom could wake the dead...
Again.

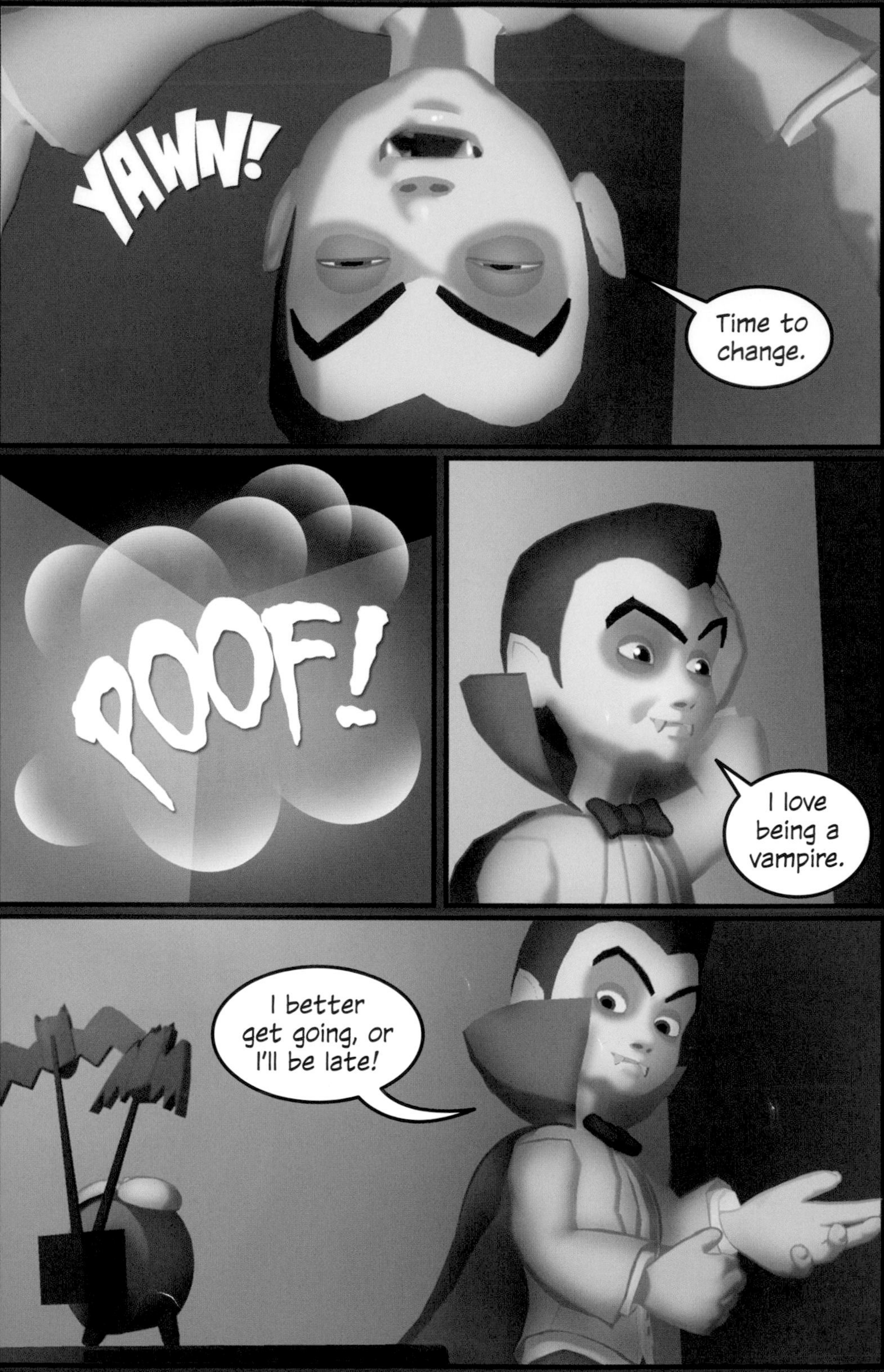
YAWN!
Time to change.
POOF!
I love being a vampire.
I better get going, or I'll be late!

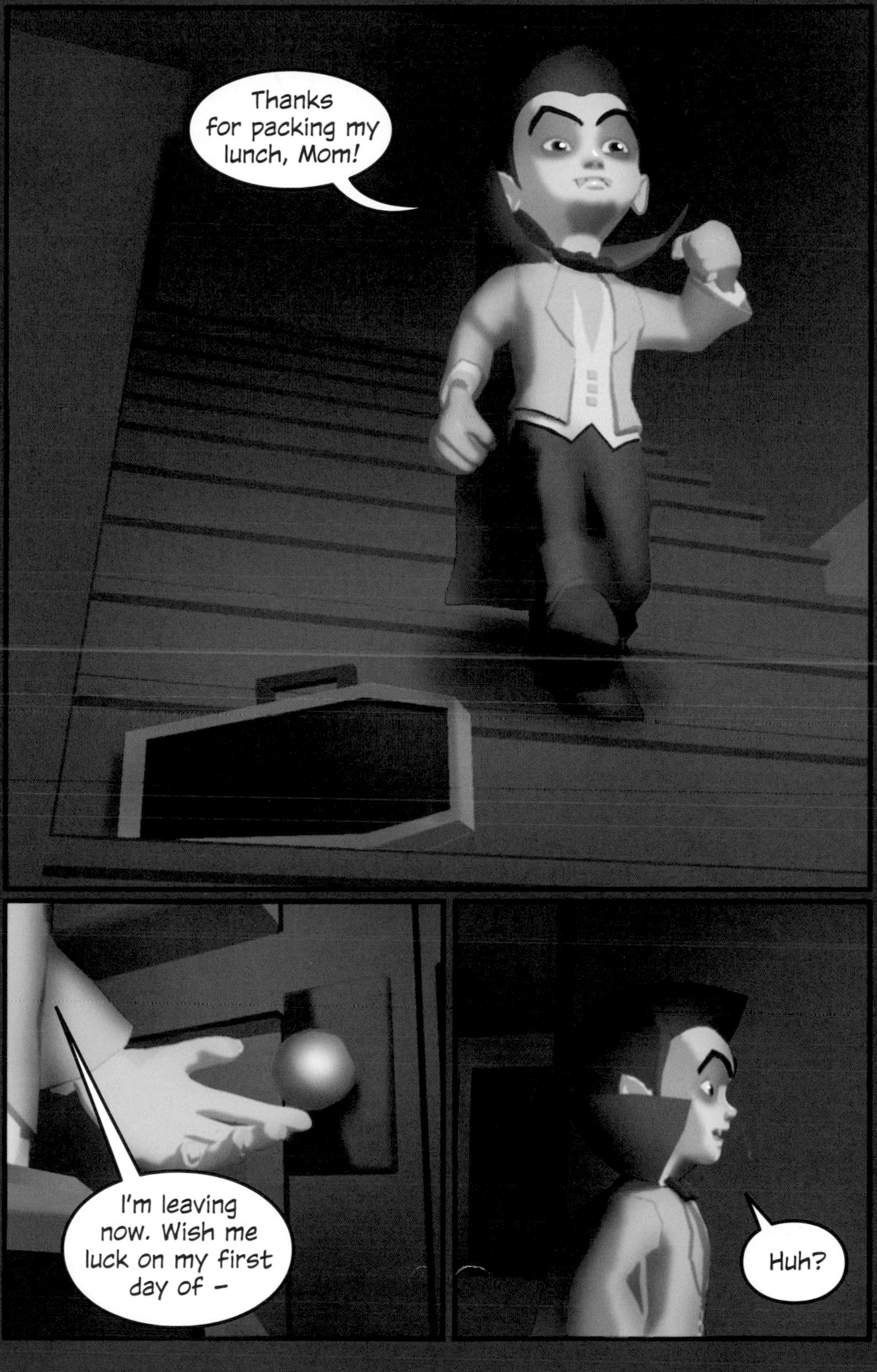
Thanks for packing my lunch, Mom!
I'm leaving now. Wish me luck on my first day of –
Huh?

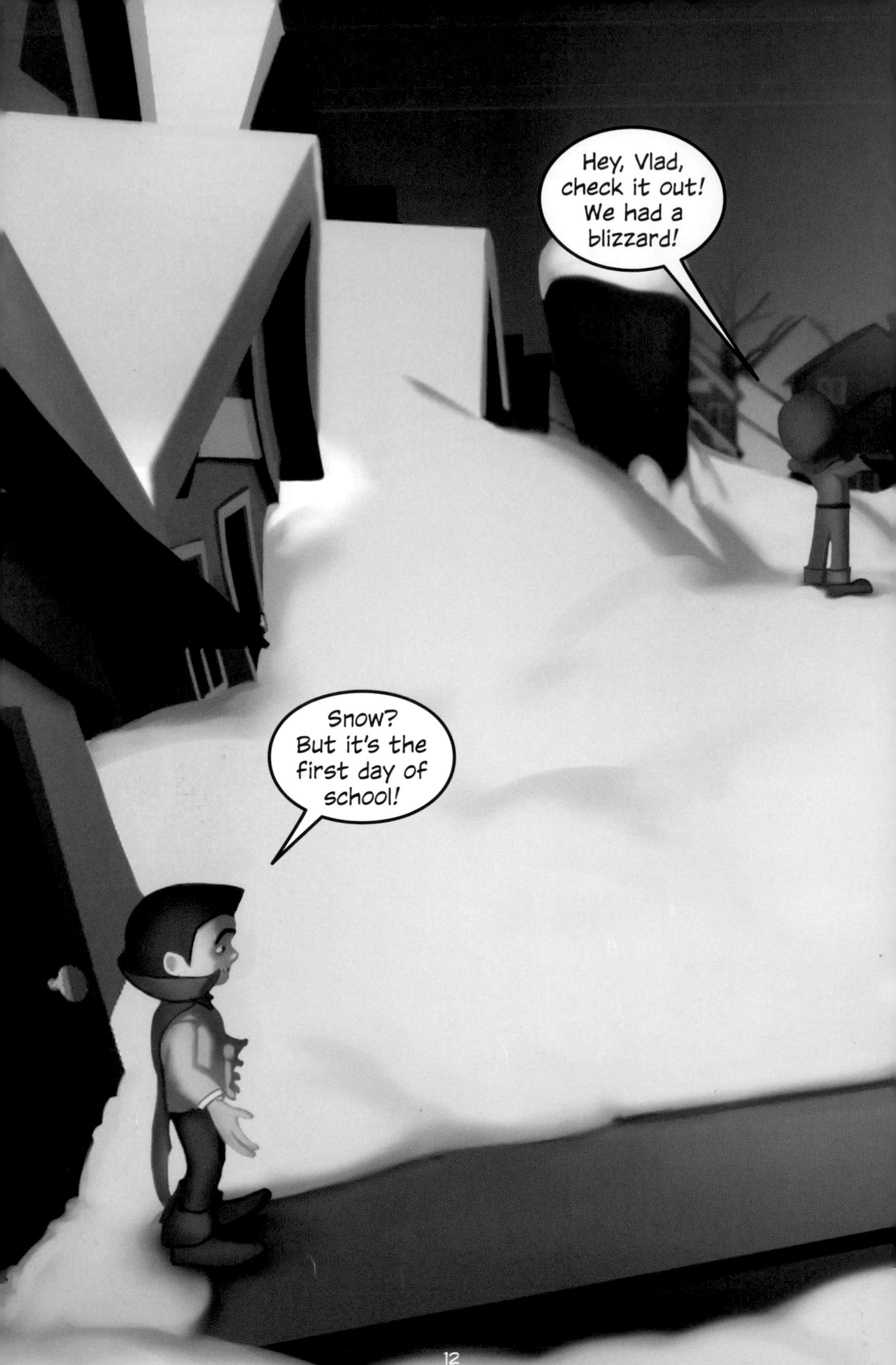
Hey, Vlad, check it out! We had a blizzard!
Snow? But it's the first day of school!

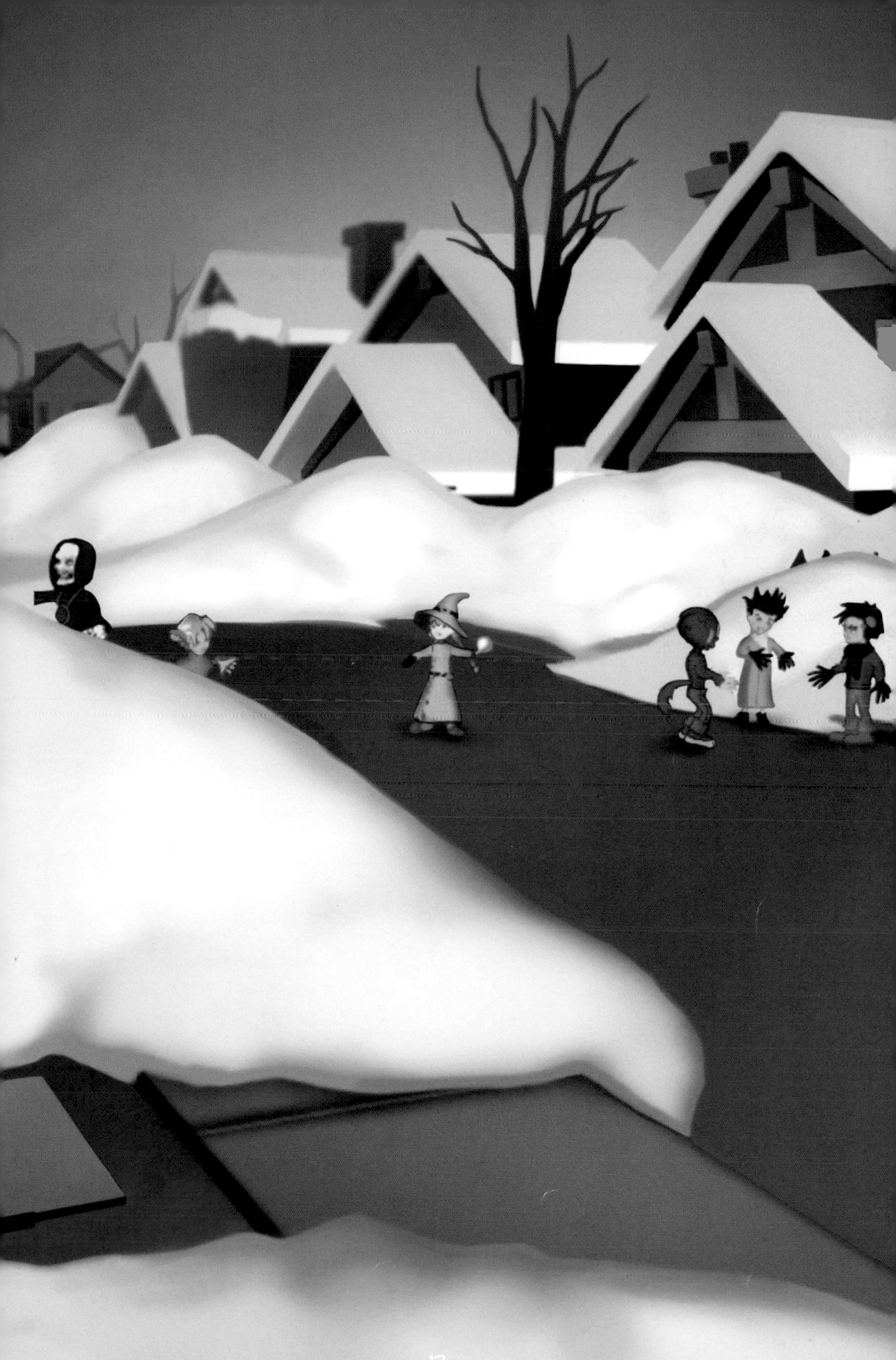

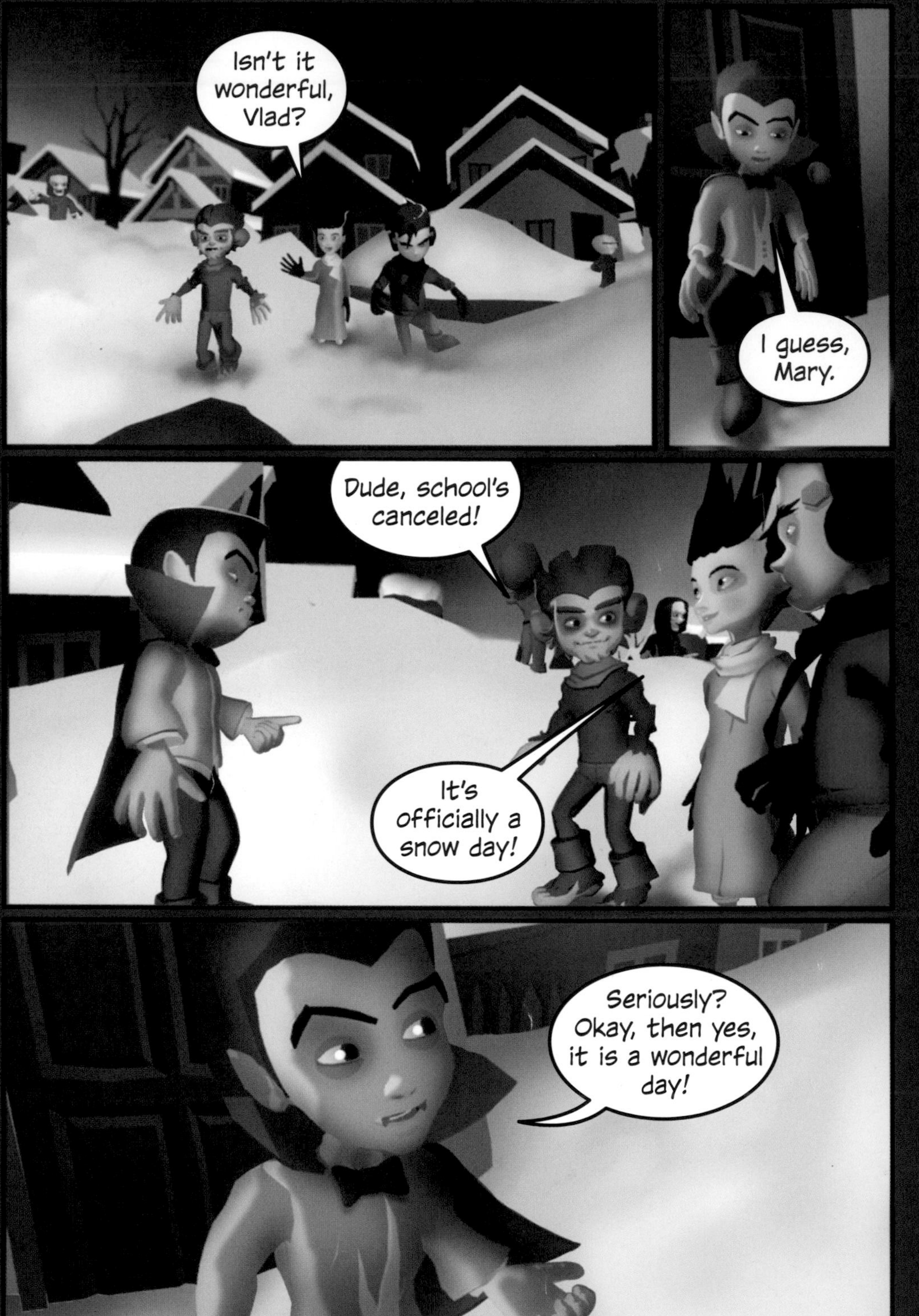
Isn't it wonderful, Vlad?
I guess, Mary.
Dude, school's canceled!
It's officially a snow day!
Seriously? Okay, then yes, it is a wonderful day!

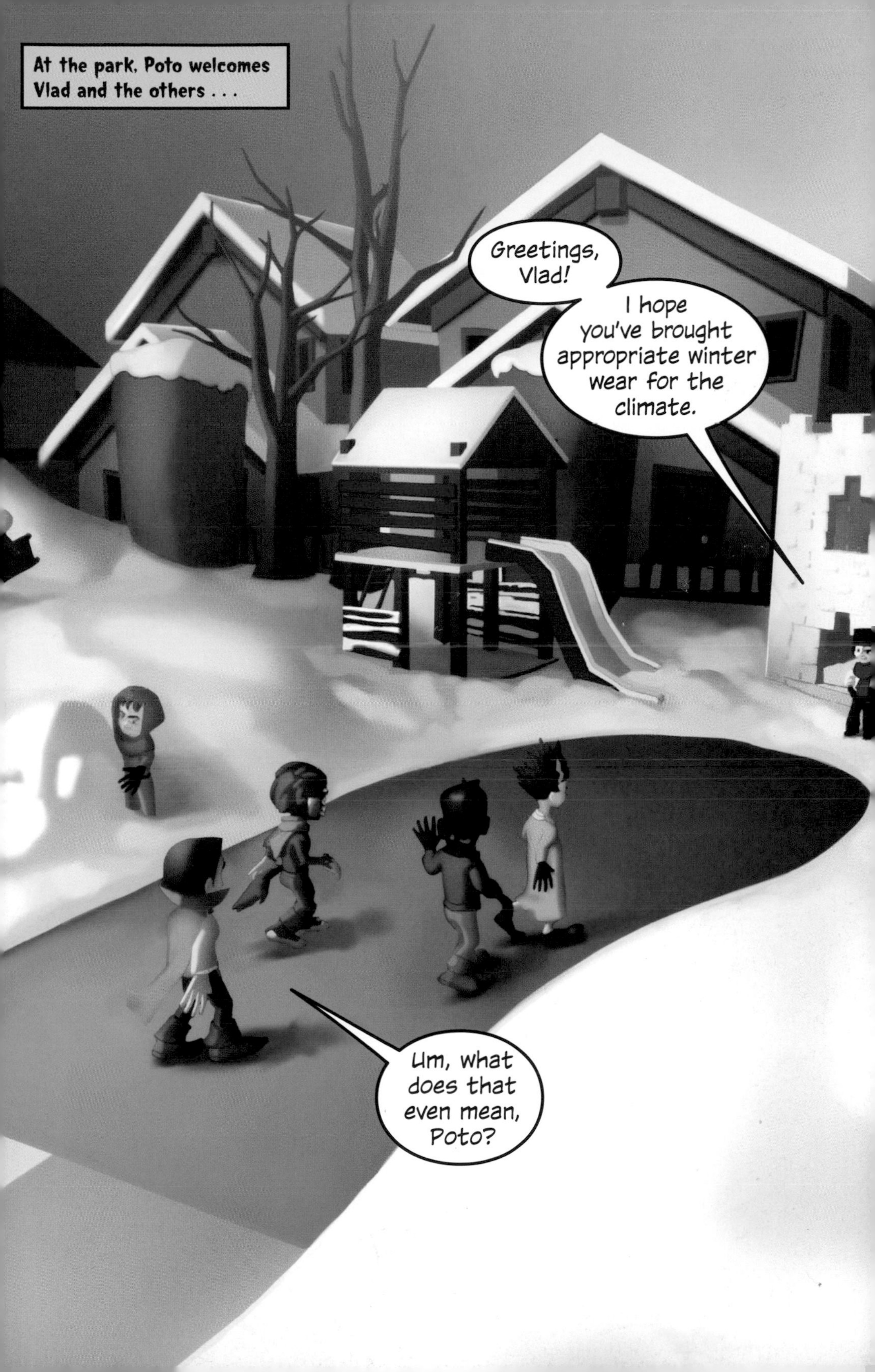
At the park, Poto welcomes Vlad and the others . . .
Greetings, Vlad!
I hope you've brought appropriate winter wear for the climate.
Um, what does that even mean, Poto?

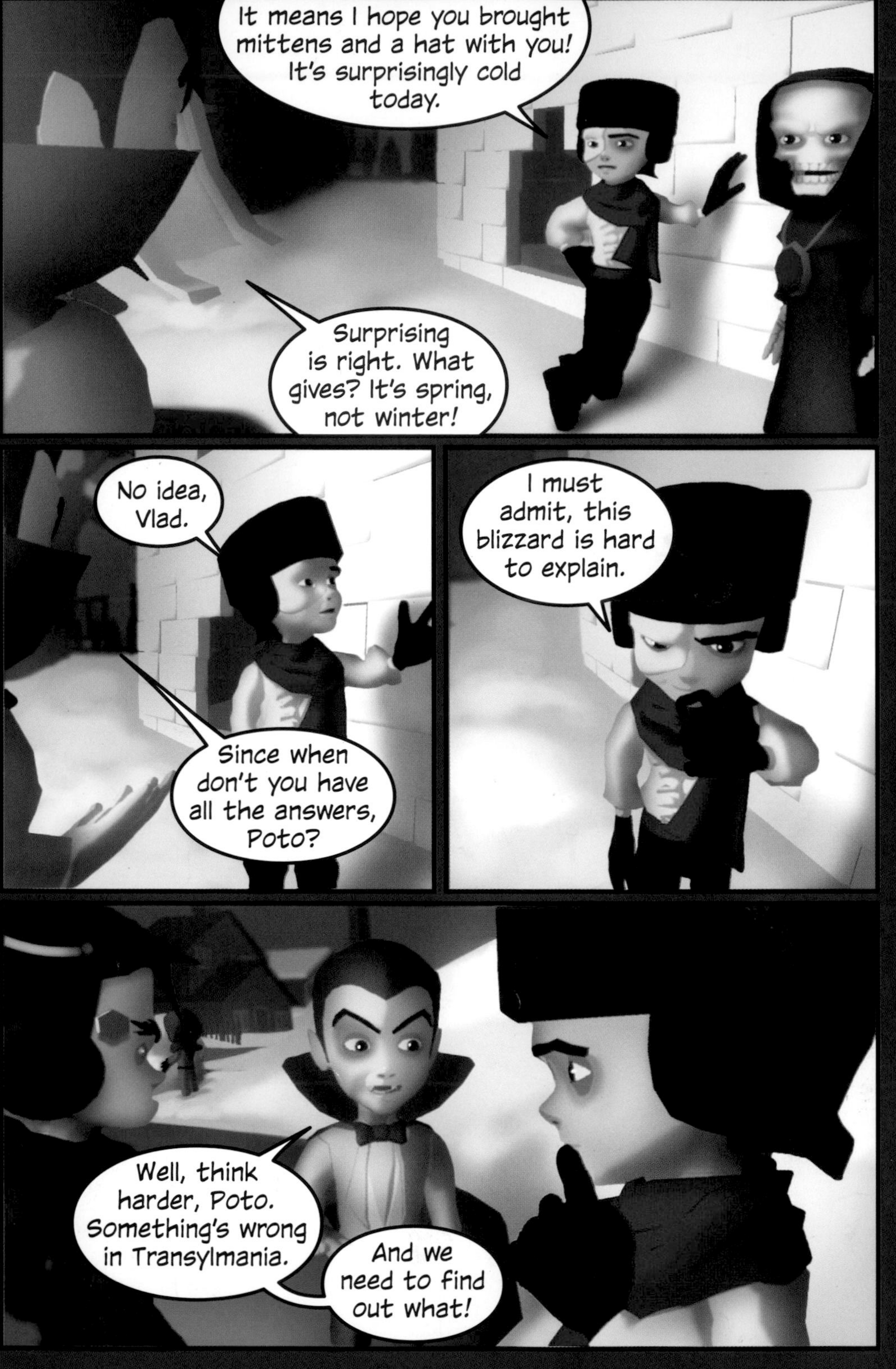
It means I hope you brought mittens and a hat with you! It's surprisingly cold today.
Surprising is right. What gives? It's spring, not winter!
No idea, Vlad.
Since when don't you have all the answers, Poto?
I must admit, this blizzard is hard to explain.
Well, think harder, Poto. Something's wrong in Transylmania.
And we need to find out what!

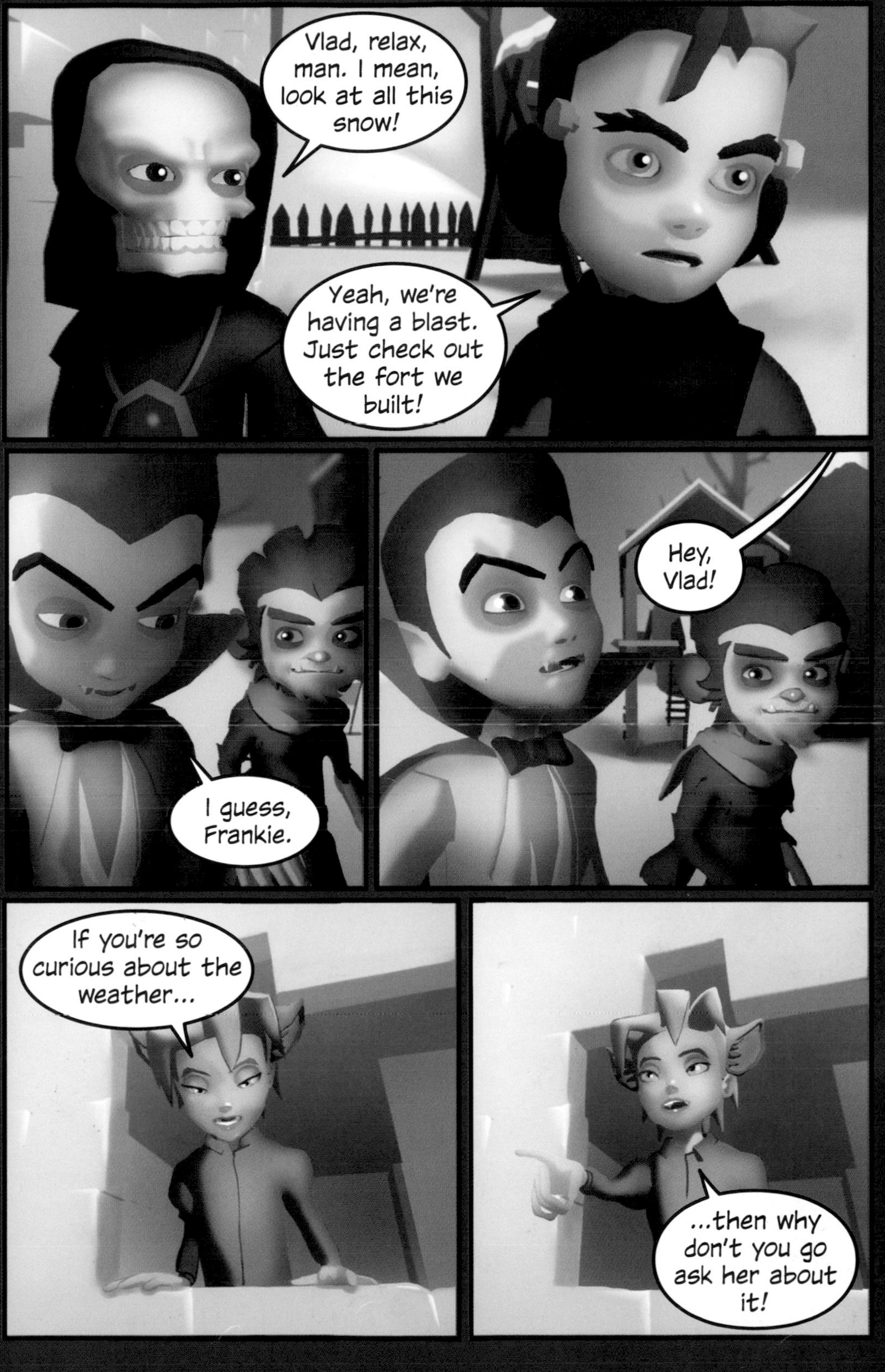
Vlad, relax, man. I mean, look at all this snow!
Yeah, we're having a blast. Just check out the fort we built!
I guess, Frankie.
Hey, Vlad!
If you're so curious about the weather...
...then why don't you go ask her about it!

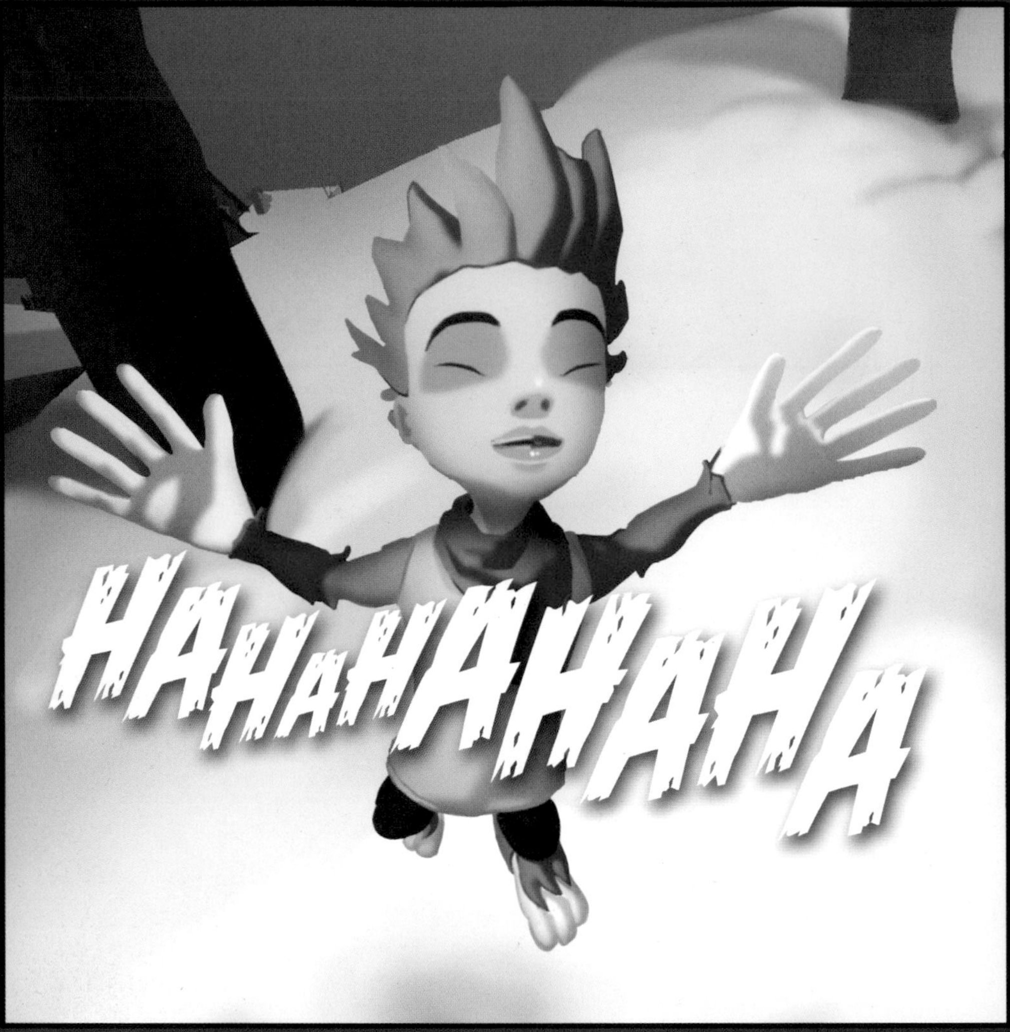
HAHAHAHAHAHA

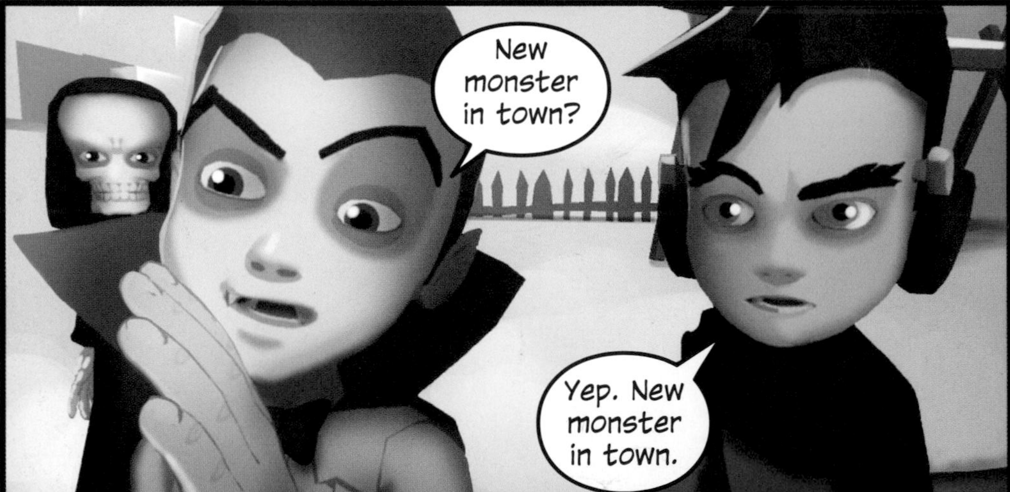
New monster in town?
Yep. New monster in town.

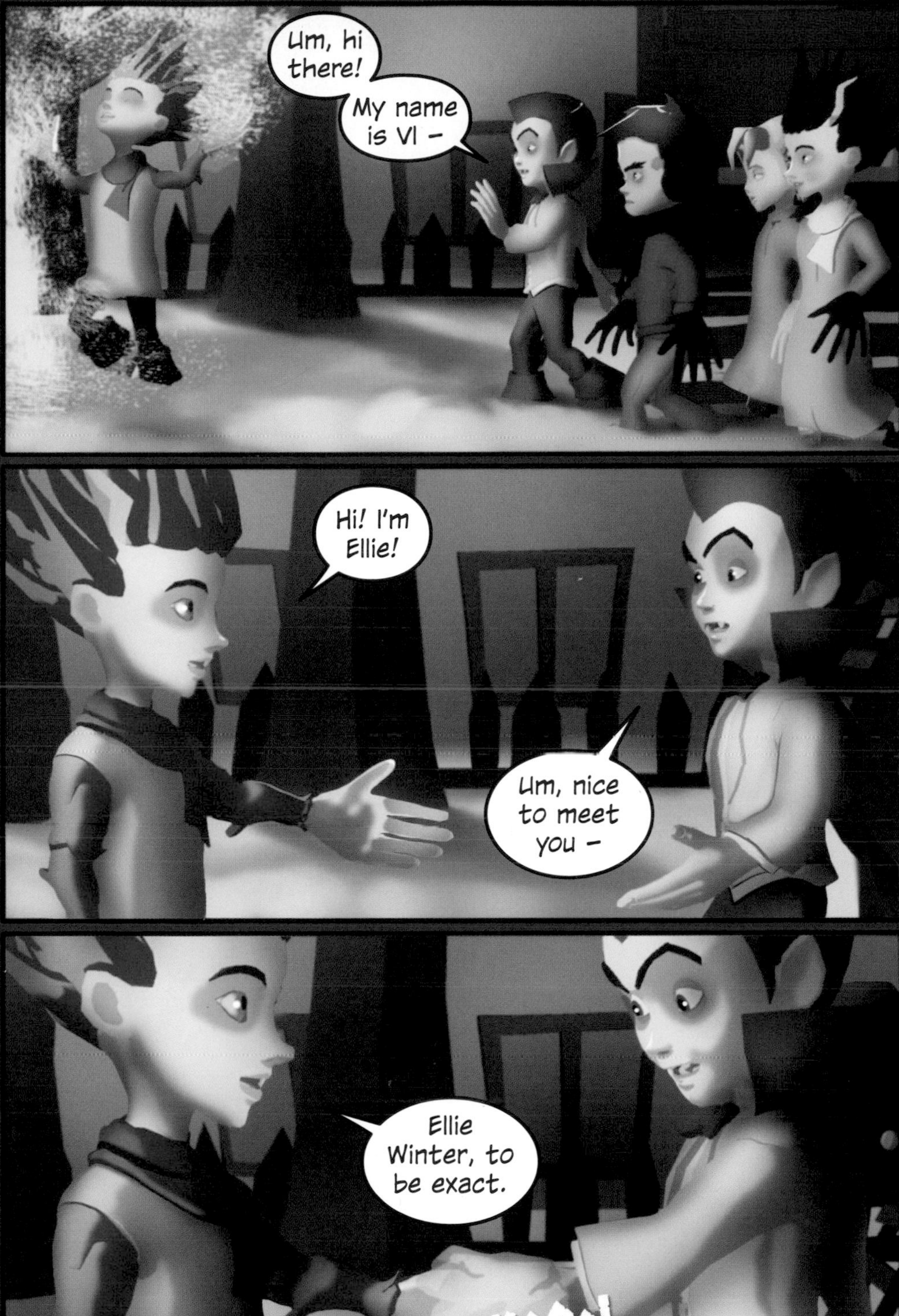
Um, hi there!
My name is Vl –
Hi! I'm Ellie!
Um, nice to meet you –
Ellie Winter, to be exact.
KRRR!

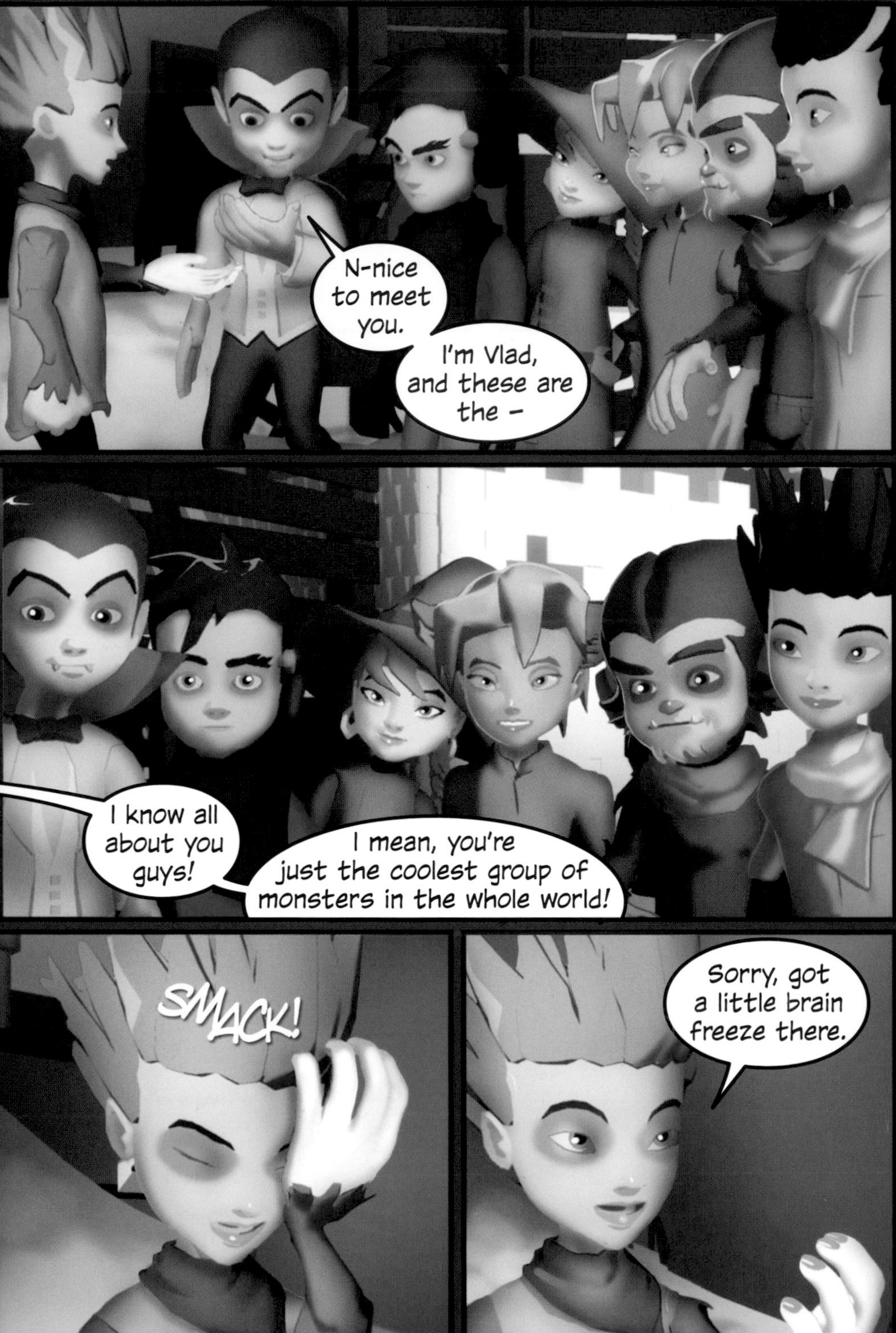
N-nice to meet you.
I'm Vlad, and these are the –
I know all about you guys!
I mean, you're just the coolest group of monsters in the whole world!
SMACK!
Sorry, got a little brain freeze there.

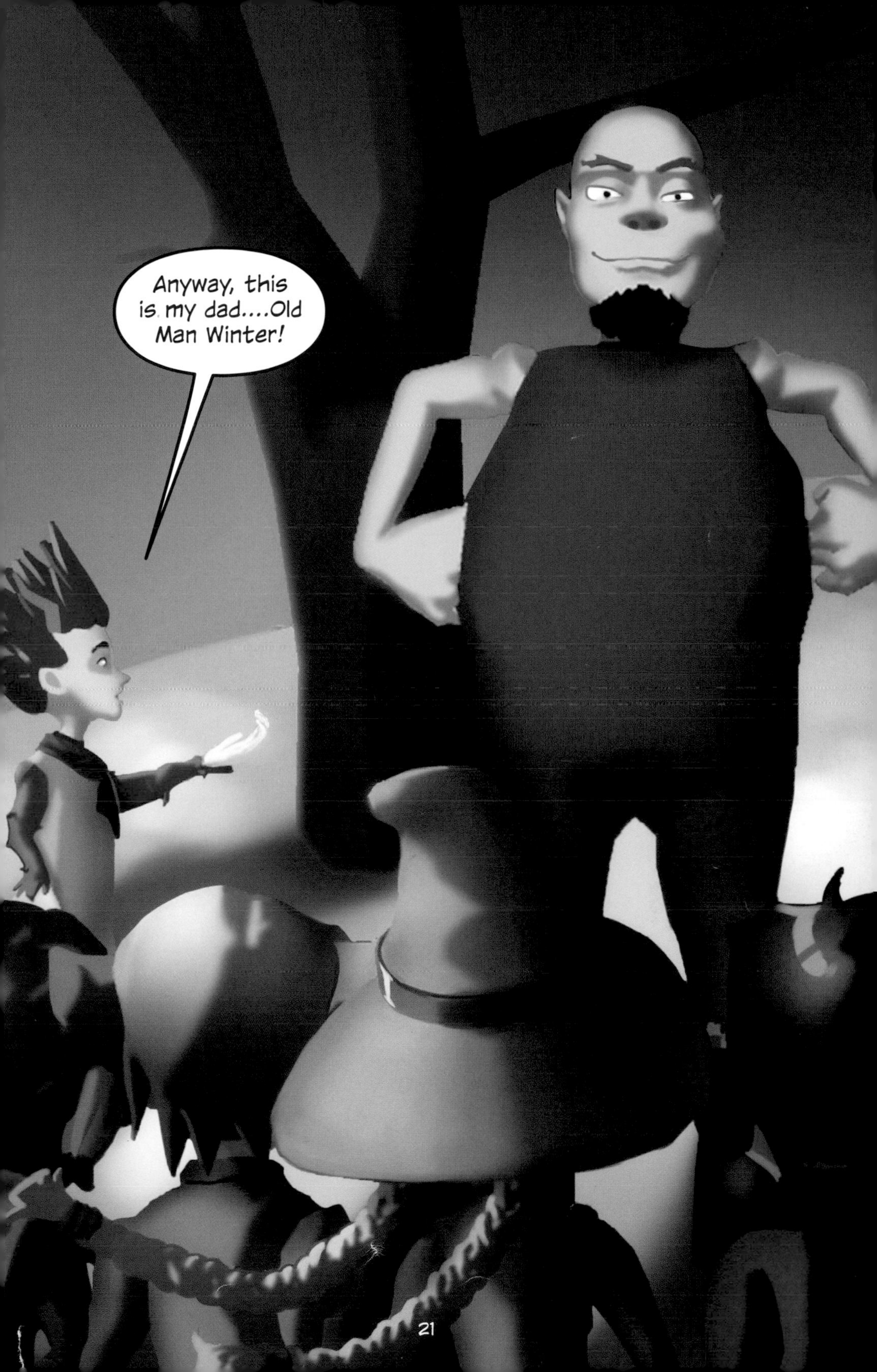
Anyway, this is my dad....Old Man Winter!

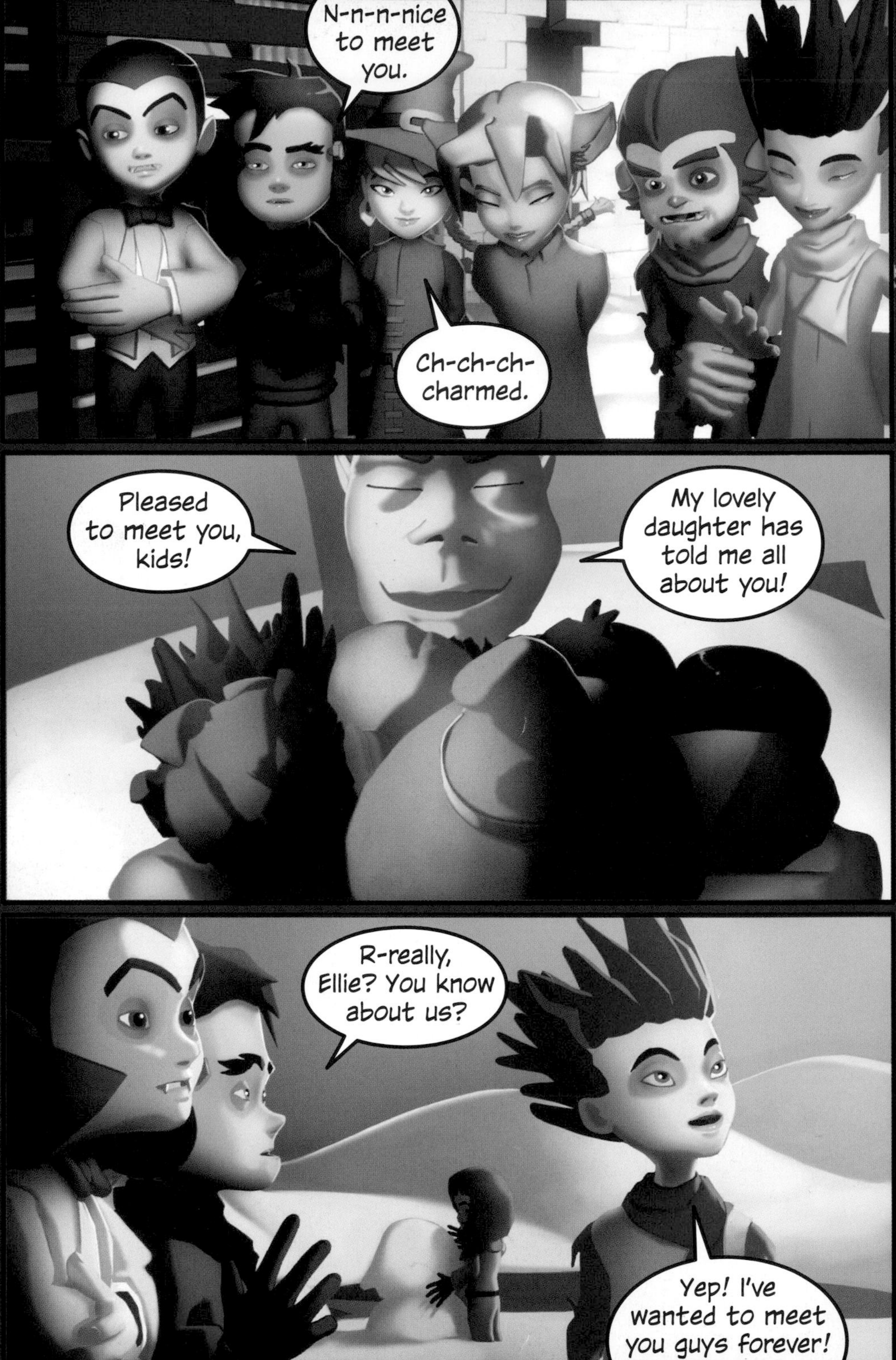
N-n-n-nice to meet you.
Ch-ch-ch-charmed.
Pleased to meet you, kids!
My lovely daughter has told me all about you!
R-really, Ellie? You know about us?
Yep! I've wanted to meet you guys forever!

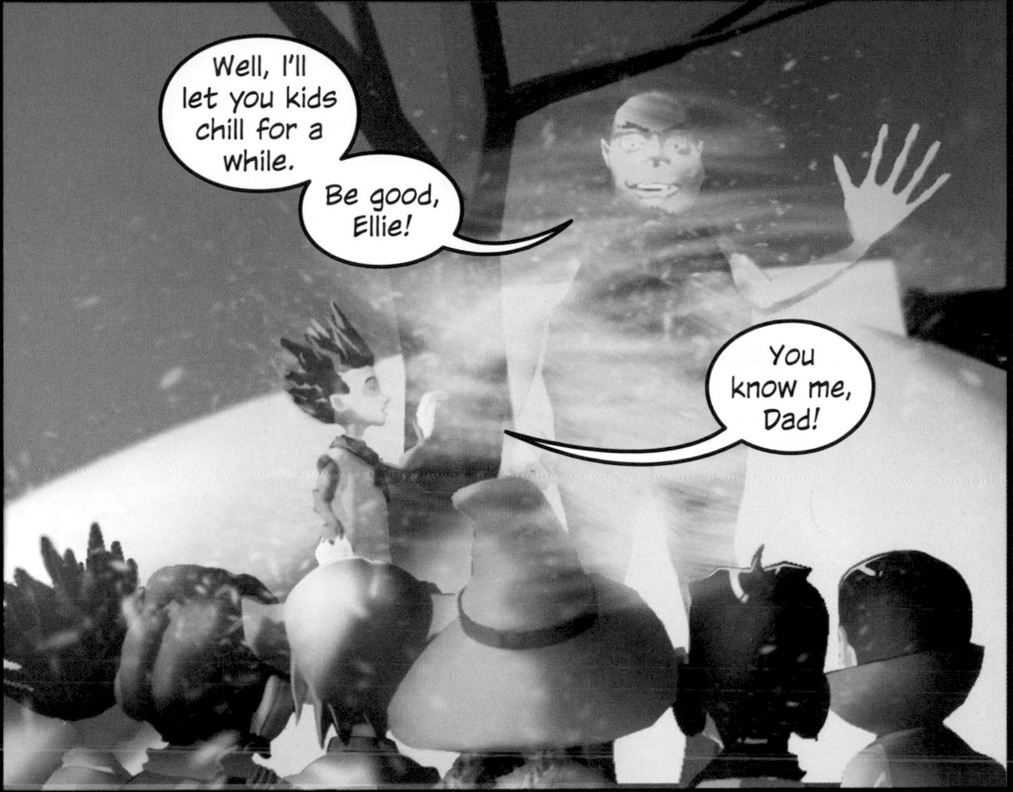
Well, I'll let you kids chill for a while.
Be good, Ellie!
You know me, Dad!

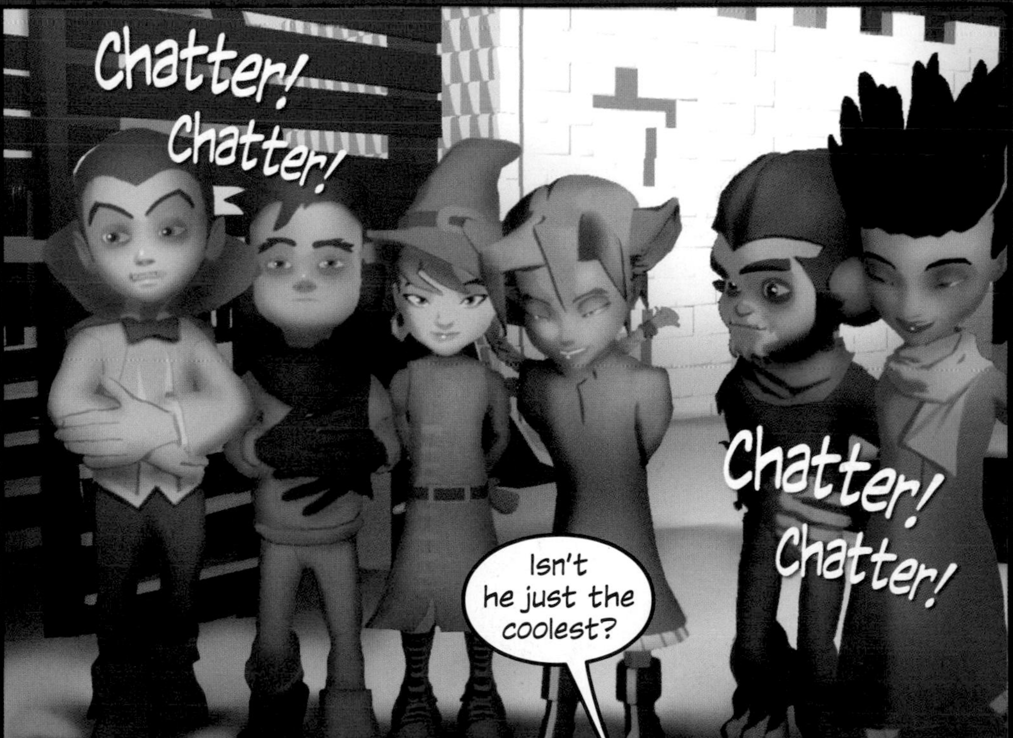
Chatter! Chatter!
Chatter! Chatter!
Isn't he just the coolest?

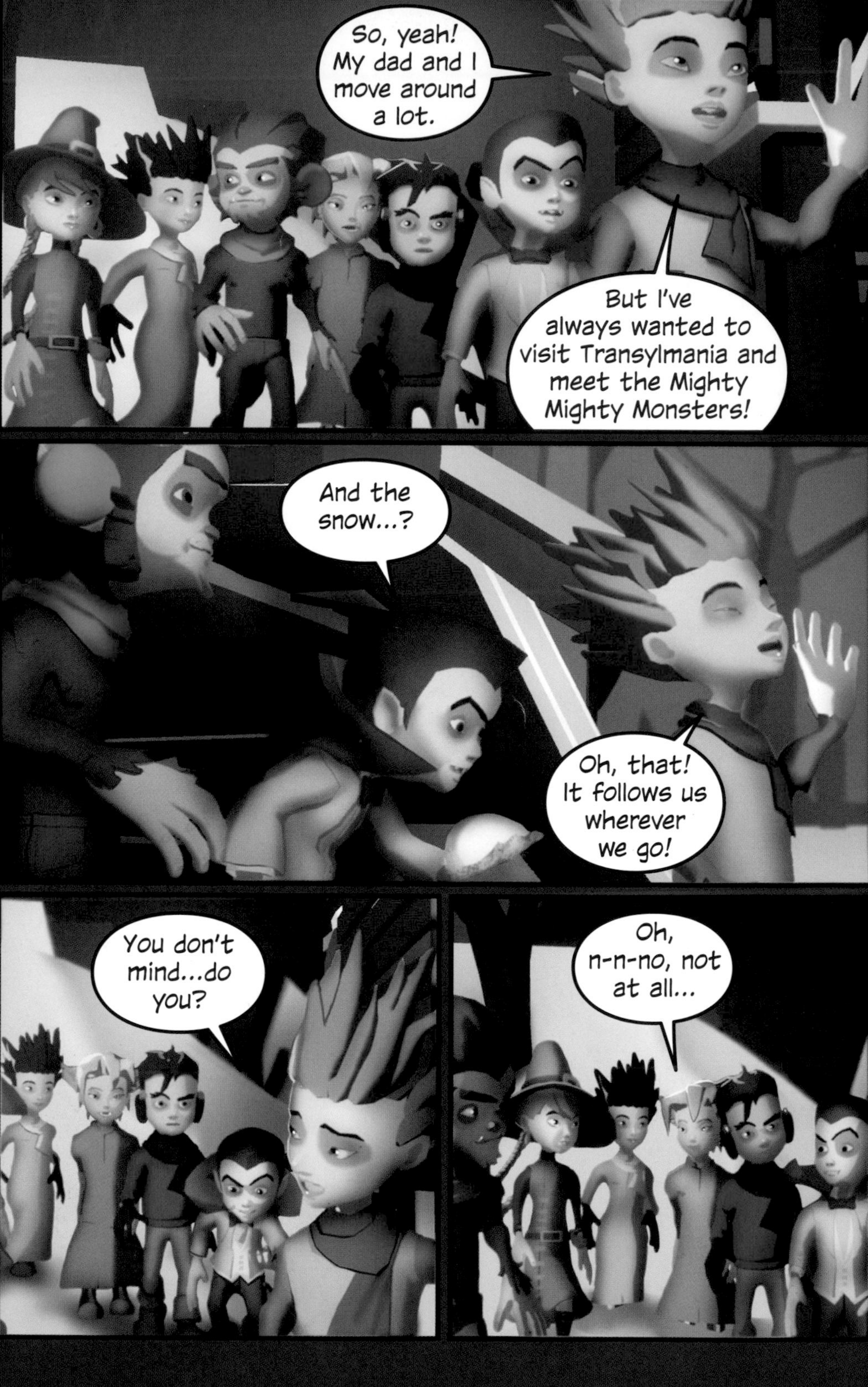
So, yeah! My dad and I move around a lot.
But I've always wanted to visit Transylmania and meet the Mighty Mighty Monsters!
And the snow...?
Oh, that! It follows us wherever we go!
You don't mind...do you?
Oh, n-n-no, not at all...

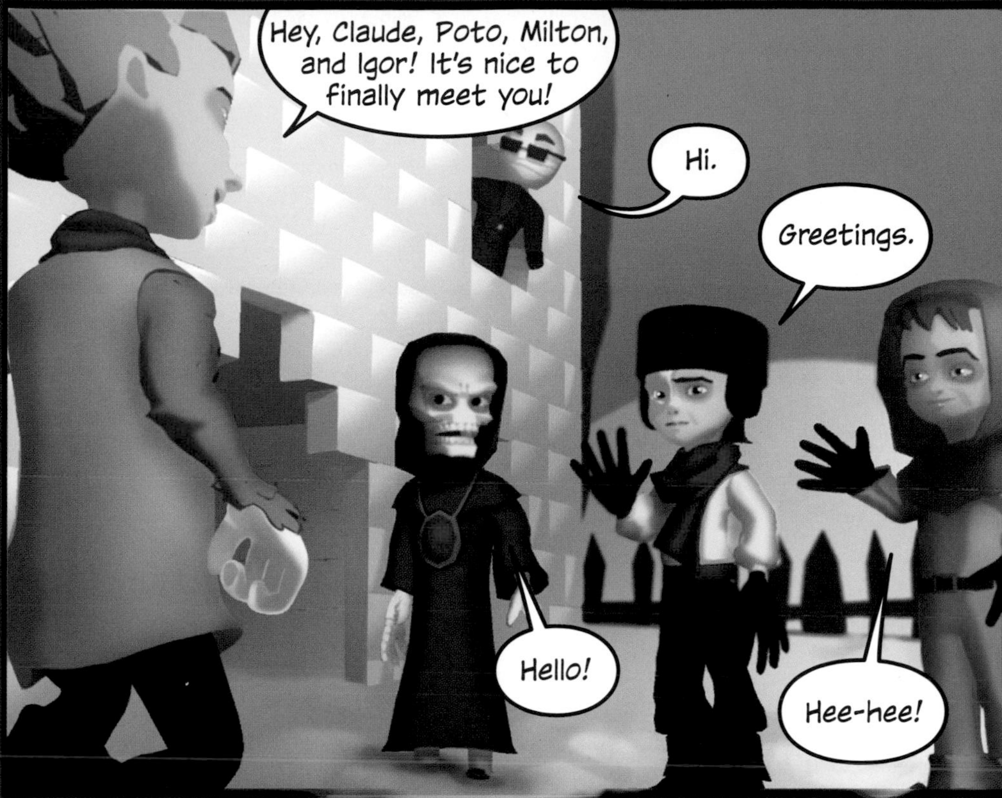
Hey, Claude, Poto, Milton, and Igor! It's nice to finally meet you!
Hi.
Greetings.
Hello!
Hee-hee!

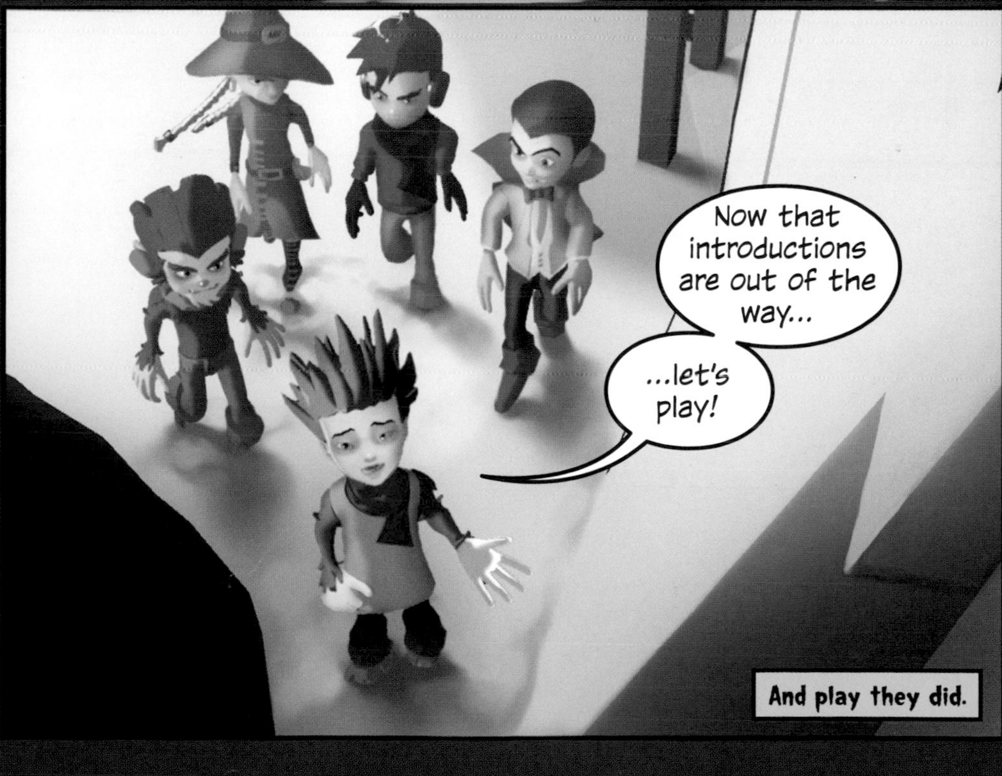
Now that introductions are out of the way...
...let's play!
And play they did.

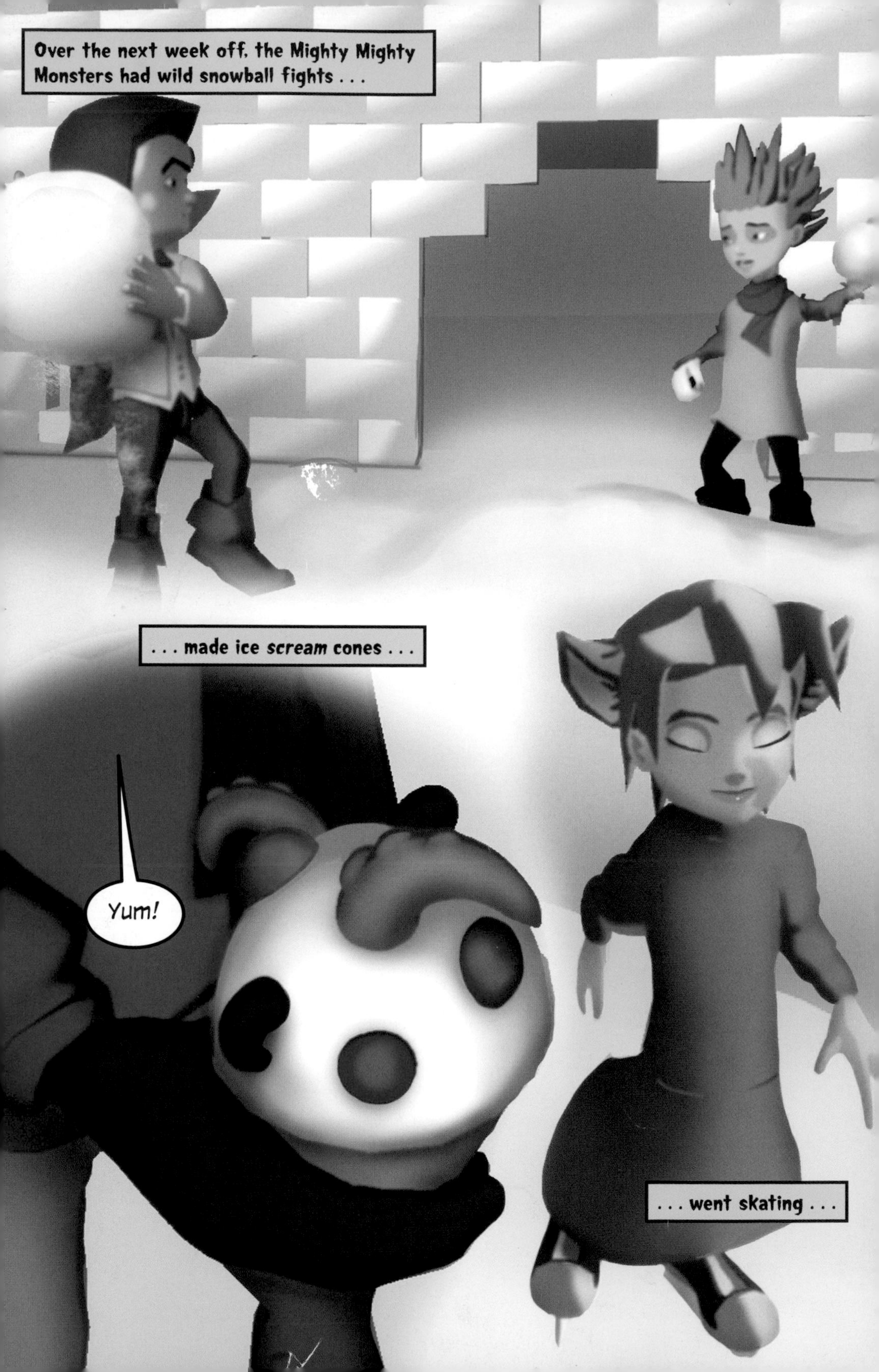
Over the next week off, the Mighty Mighty Monsters had wild snowball fights . . .
. . . made ice *scream* cones . . .
Yum!
. . . went skating . . .

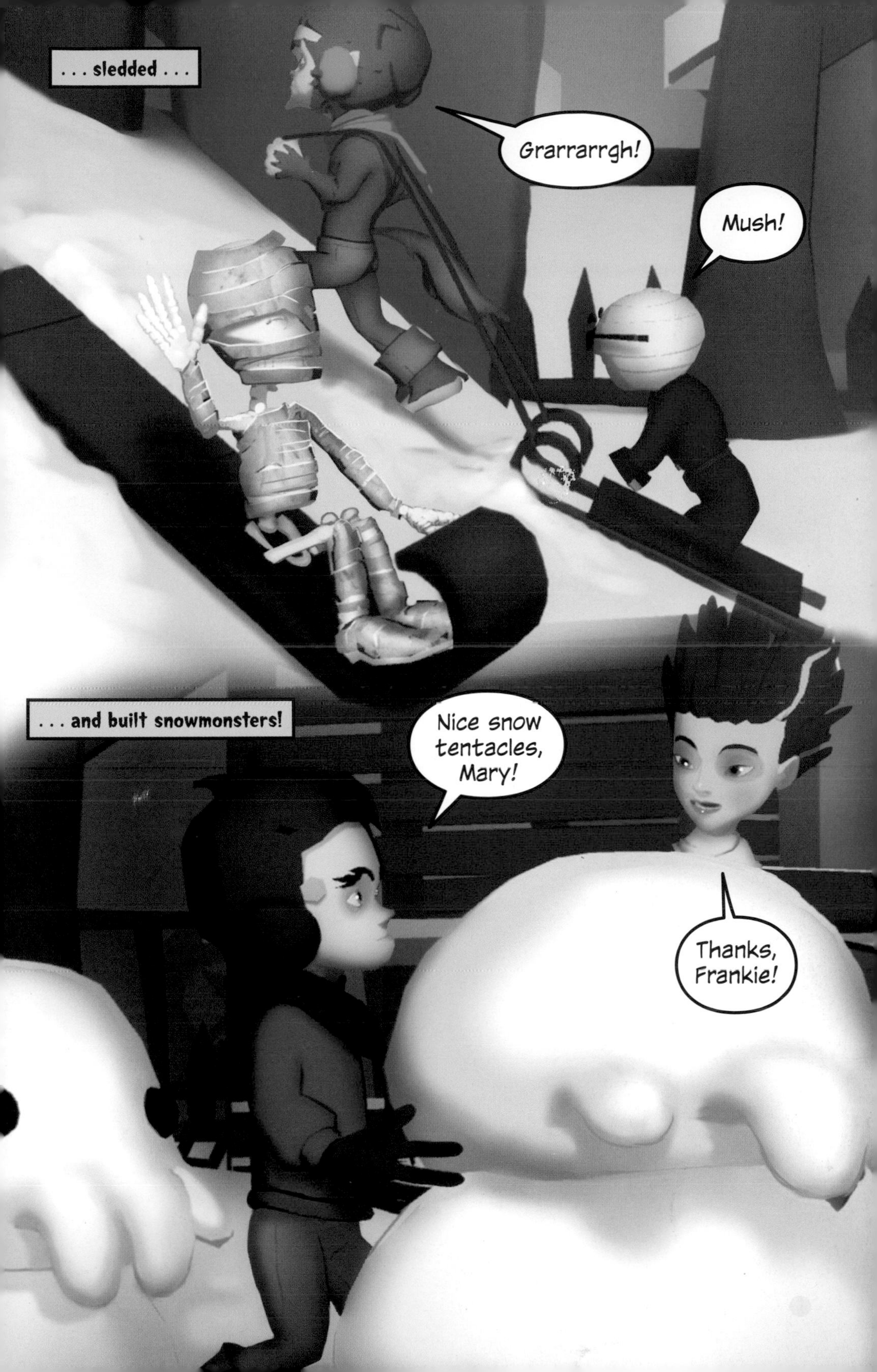
. . . sledded . . .
Grarrarrgh!
Mush!
. . . and built snowmonsters!
Nice snow tentacles, Mary!
Thanks, Frankie!

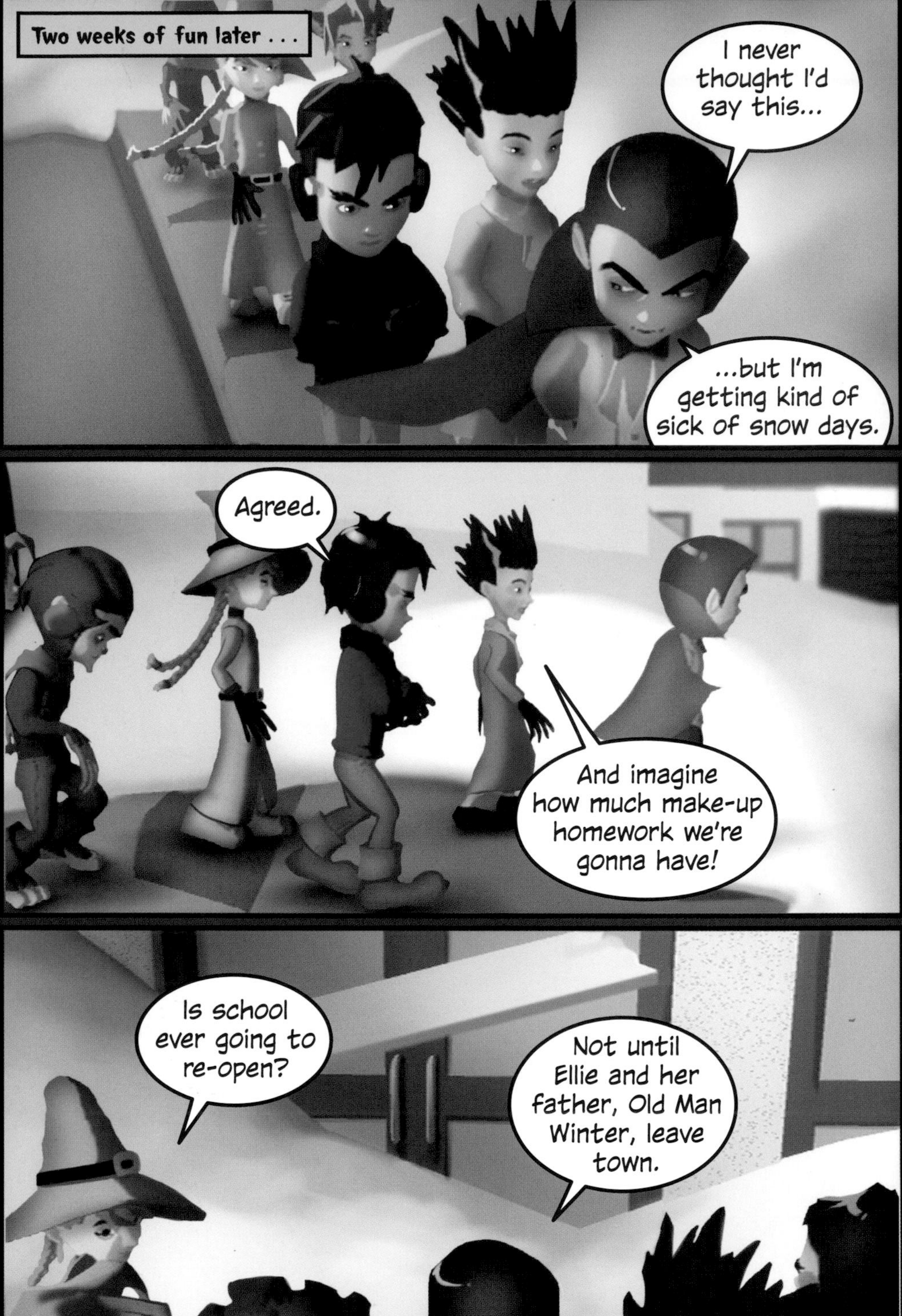
Two weeks of fun later . . .
I never thought I'd say this...
...but I'm getting kind of sick of snow days.
Agreed.
And imagine how much make-up homework we're gonna have!
Is school ever going to re-open?
Not until Ellie and her father, Old Man Winter, leave town.

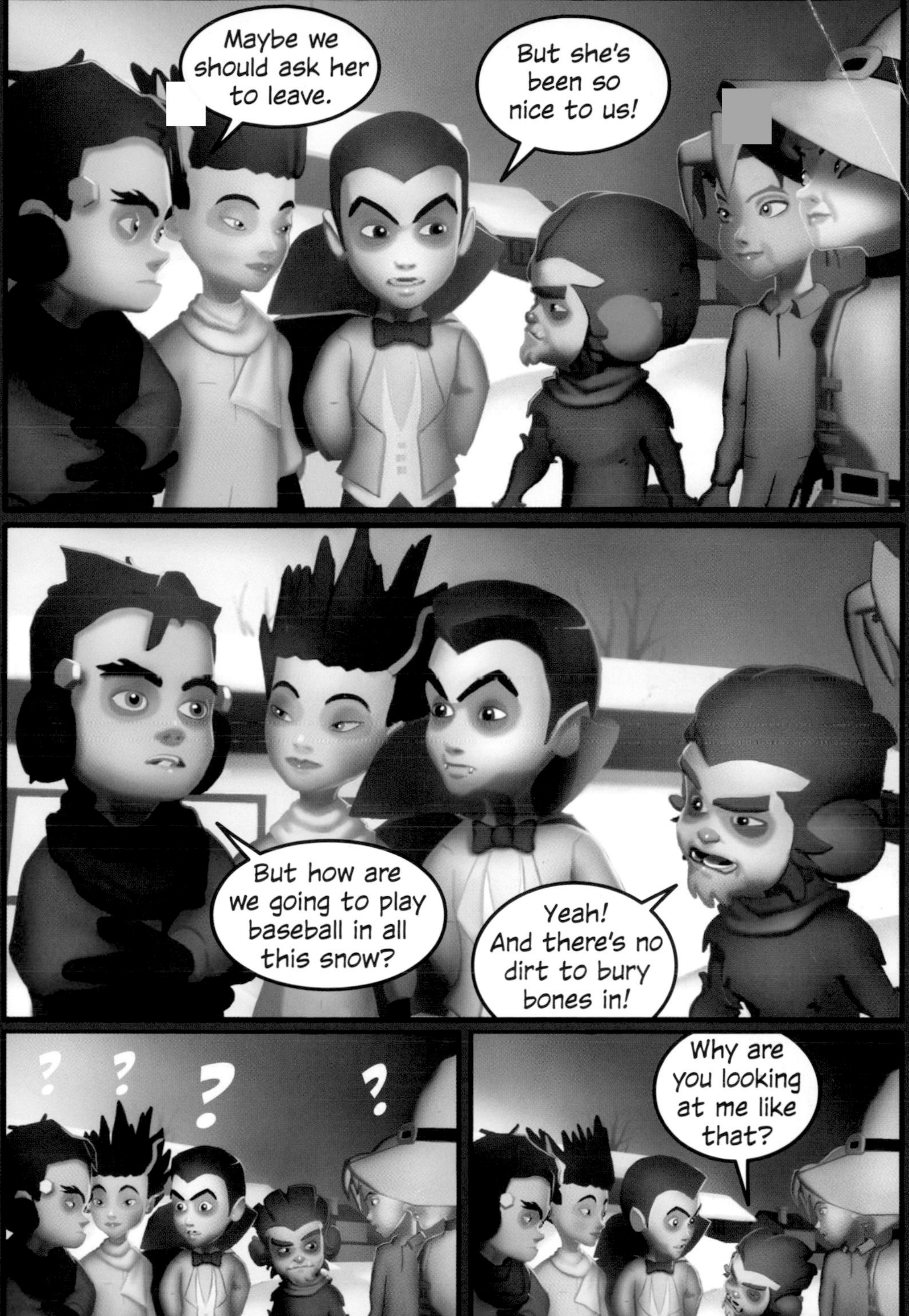
Maybe we should ask her to leave.
But she's been so nice to us!
But how are we going to play baseball in all this snow?
Yeah! And there's no dirt to bury bones in!
? ? ? ?
Why are you looking at me like that?

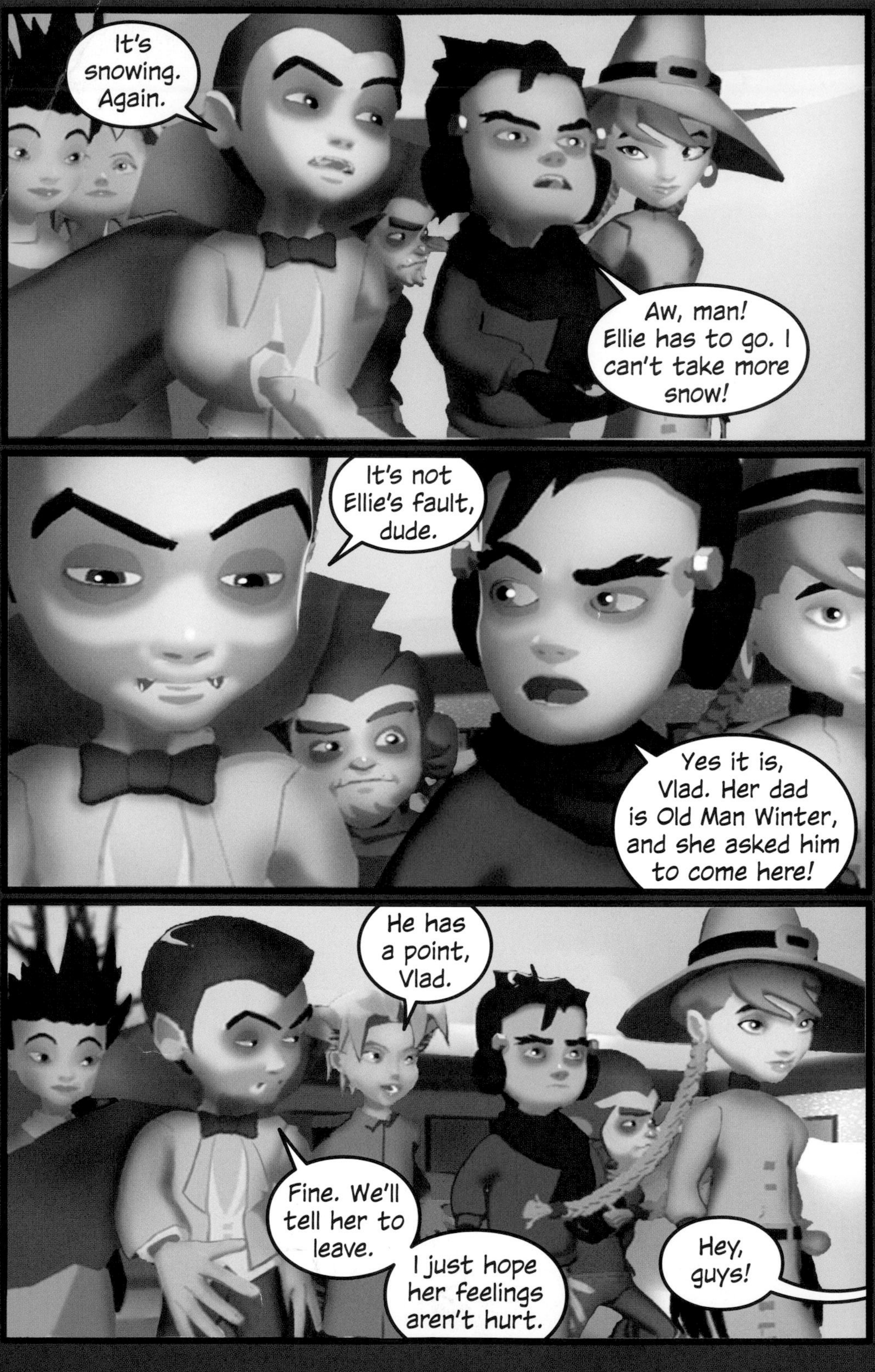
It's snowing. Again.
Aw, man! Ellie has to go. I can't take more snow!
It's not Ellie's fault, dude.
Yes it is, Vlad. Her dad is Old Man Winter, and she asked him to come here!
He has a point, Vlad.
Fine. We'll tell her to leave.
I just hope her feelings aren't hurt.
Hey, guys!

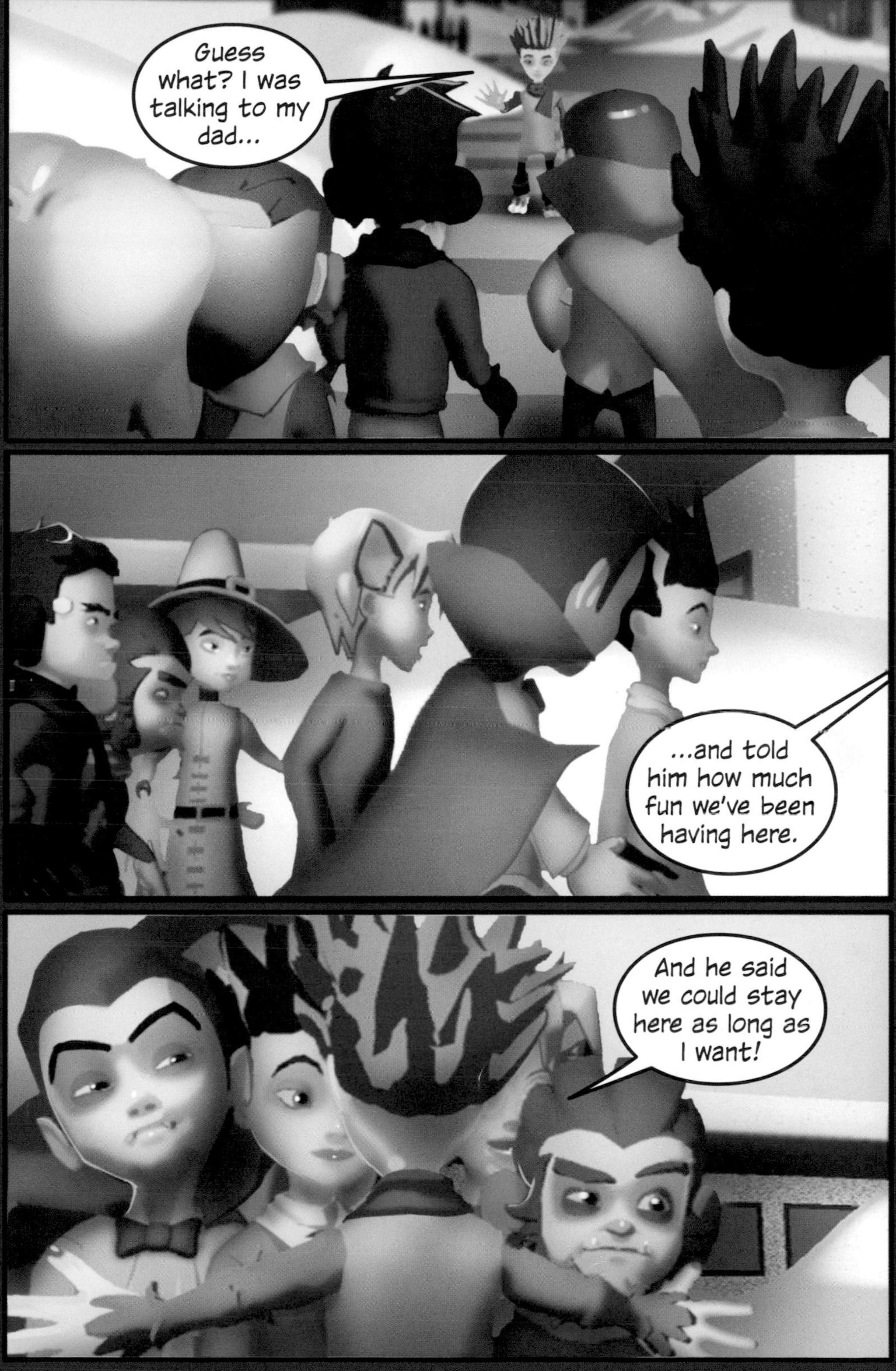
Guess what? I was talking to my dad...
...and told him how much fun we've been having here.
And he said we could stay here as long as I want!

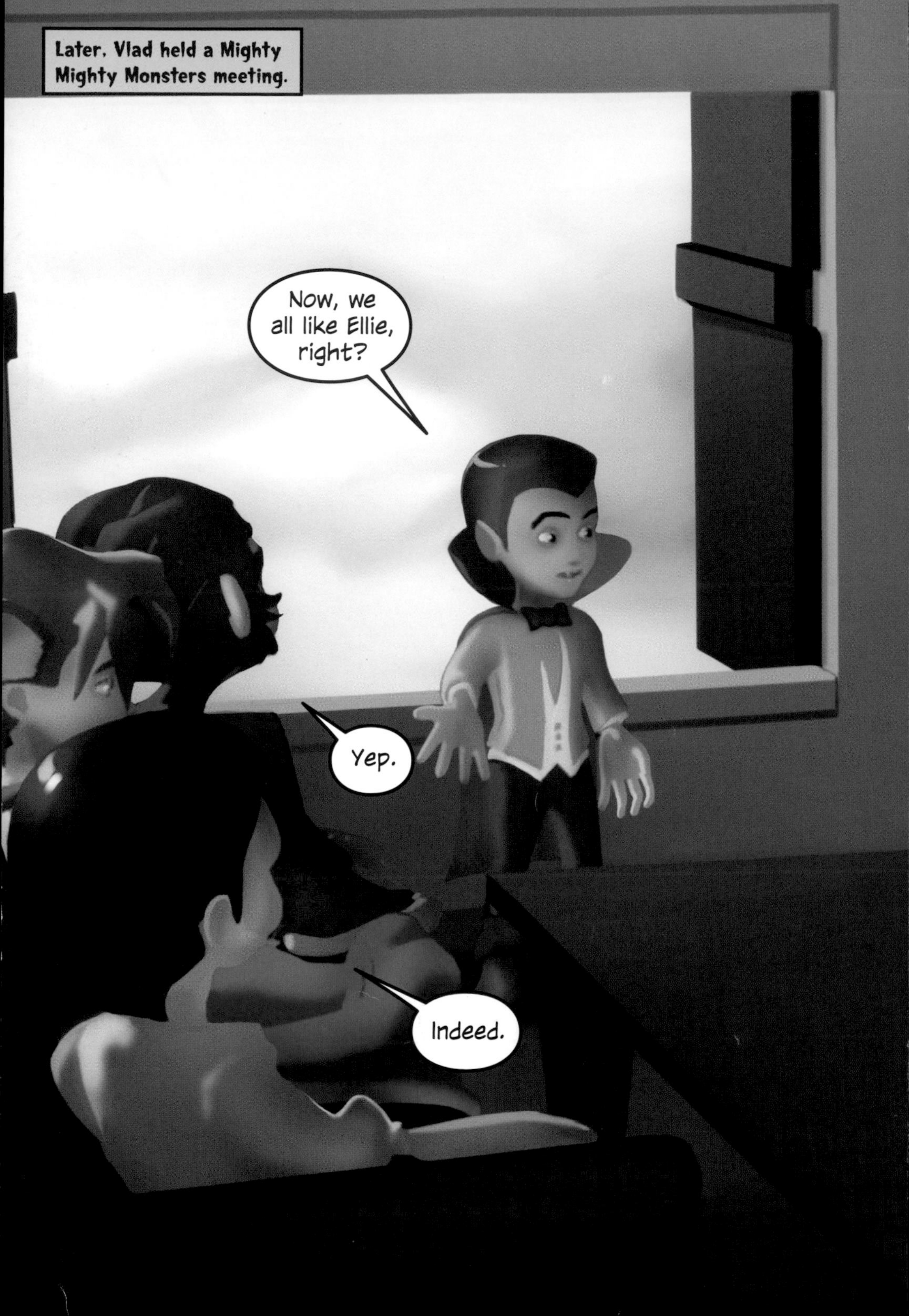
Later. Vlad held a Mighty Mighty Monsters meeting.
Now, we all like Ellie, right?
Yep.
Indeed.

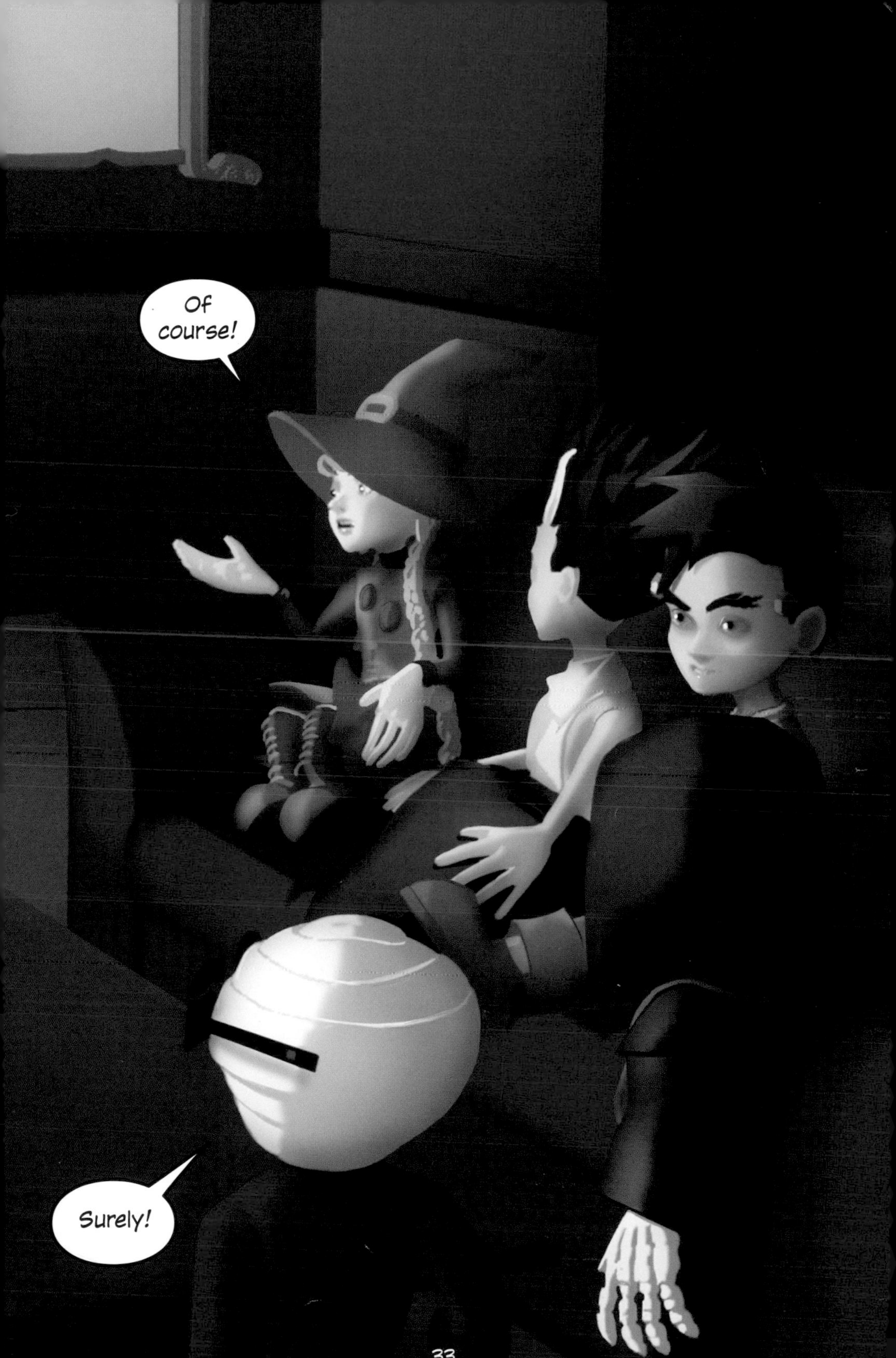
Of course!
Surely!

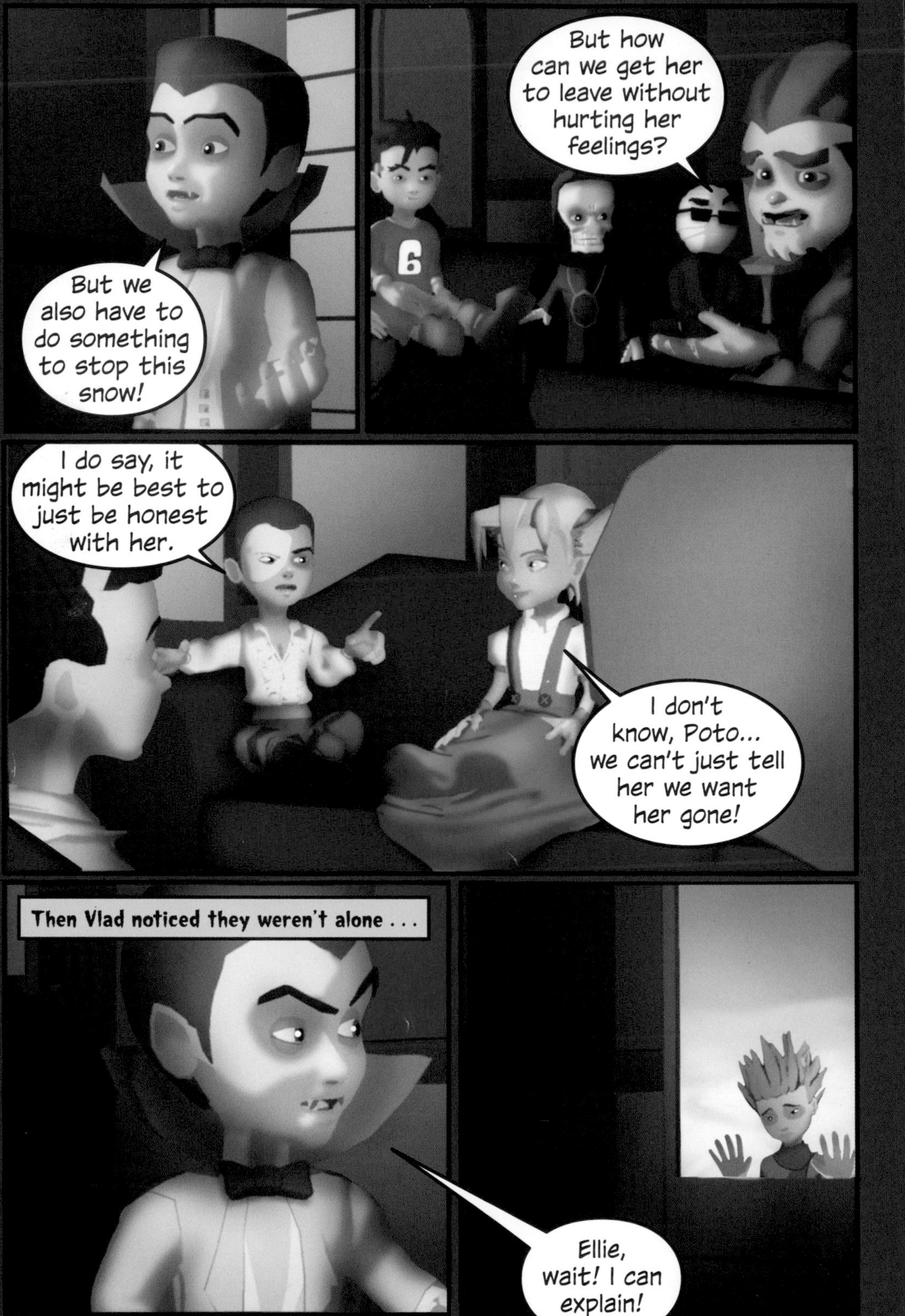

But we also have to do something to stop this snow!
But how can we get her to leave without hurting her feelings?
I do say, it might be best to just be honest with her.
I don't know, Poto... we can't just tell her we want her gone!
Then Vlad noticed they weren't alone . . .
Ellie, wait! I can explain!

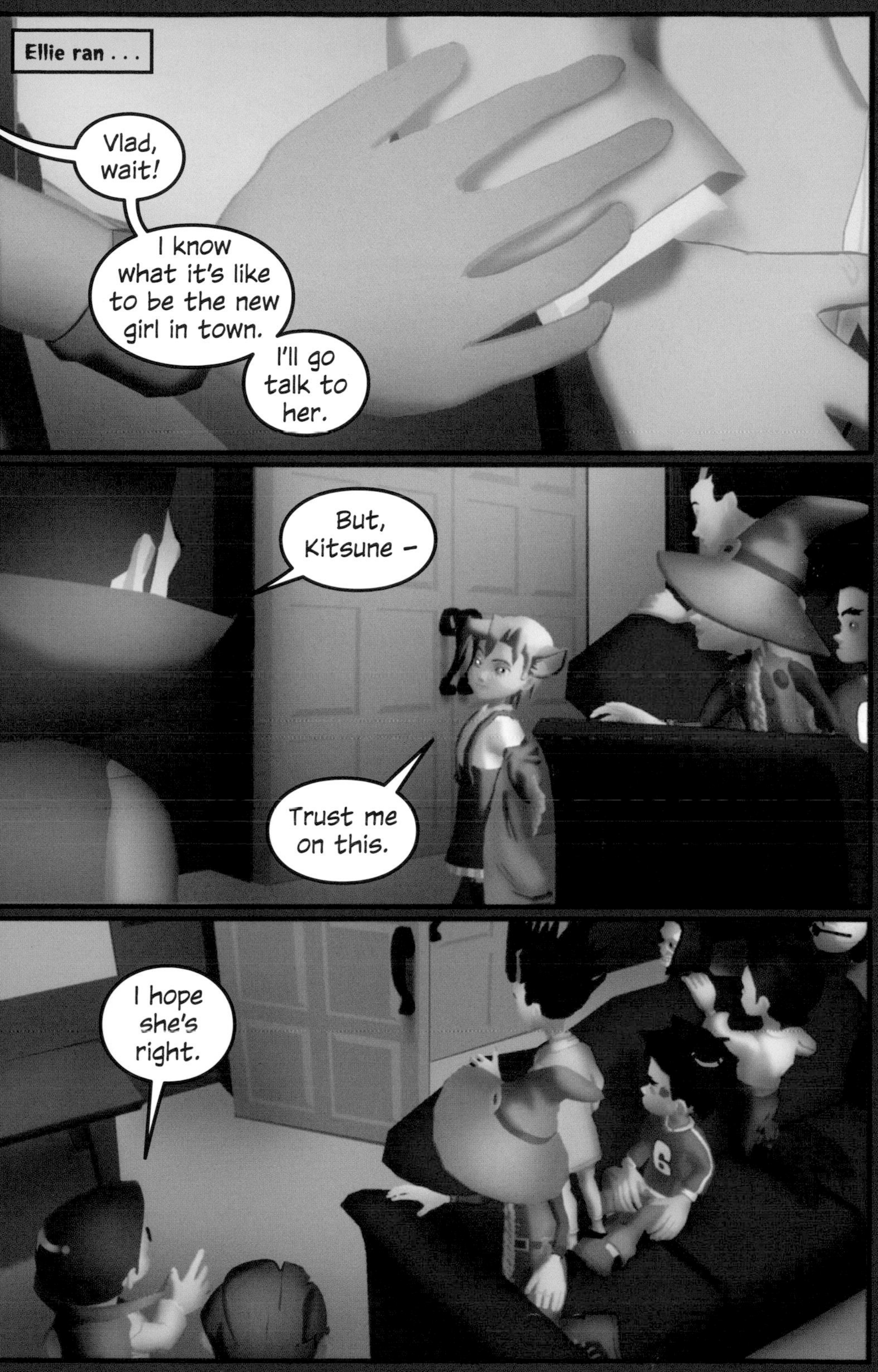
Ellie ran . . .
Vlad, wait!
I know what it's like to be the new girl in town.
I'll go talk to her.
But, Kitsune –
Trust me on this.
I hope she's right.

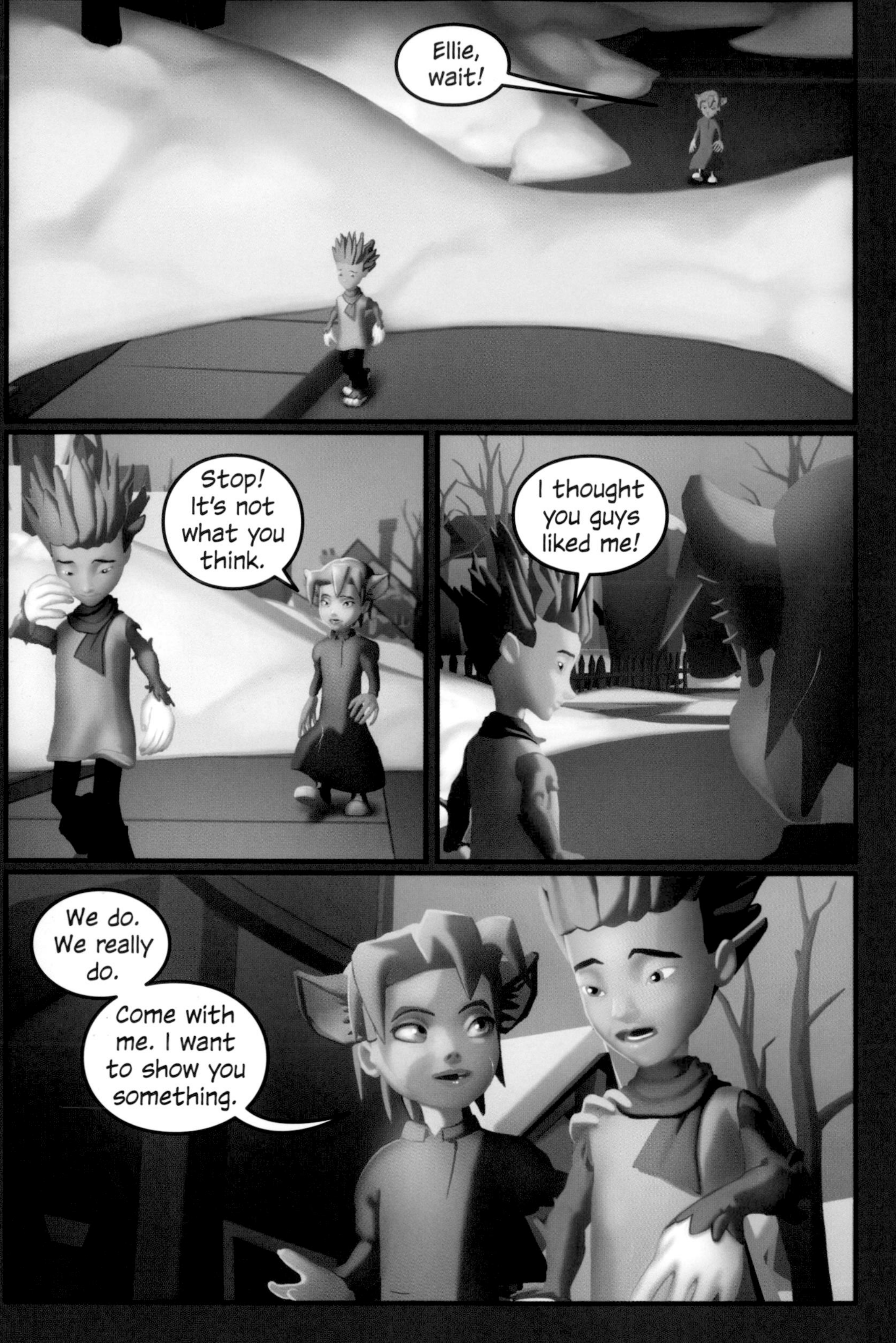
Ellie, wait!
Stop! It's not what you think.
I thought you guys liked me!
We do. We really do.
Come with me. I want to show you something.

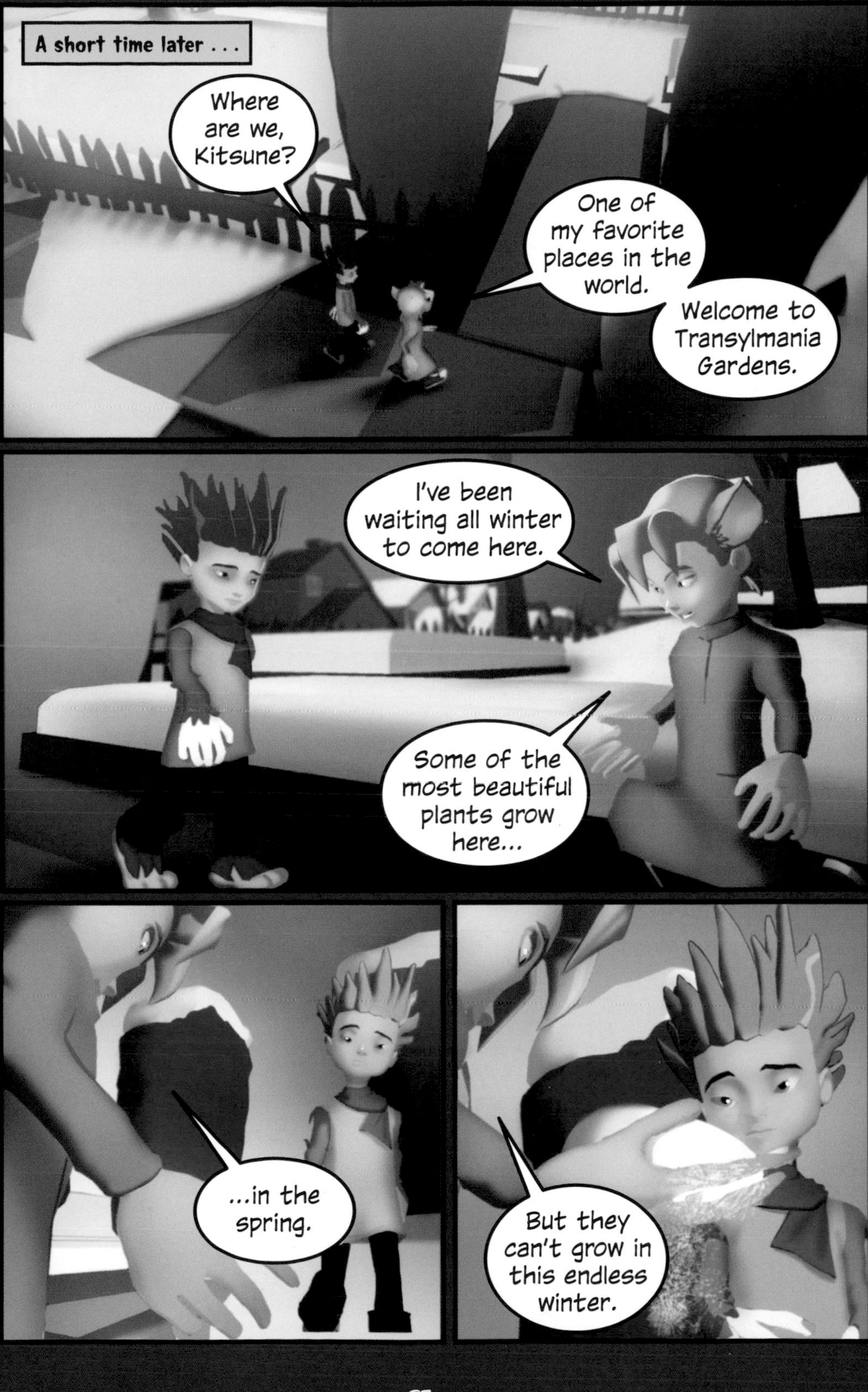
A short time later . . .
Where are we, Kitsune?
One of my favorite places in the world.
Welcome to Transylmania Gardens.
I've been waiting all winter to come here.
Some of the most beautiful plants grow here...
...in the spring.
But they can't grow in this endless winter.

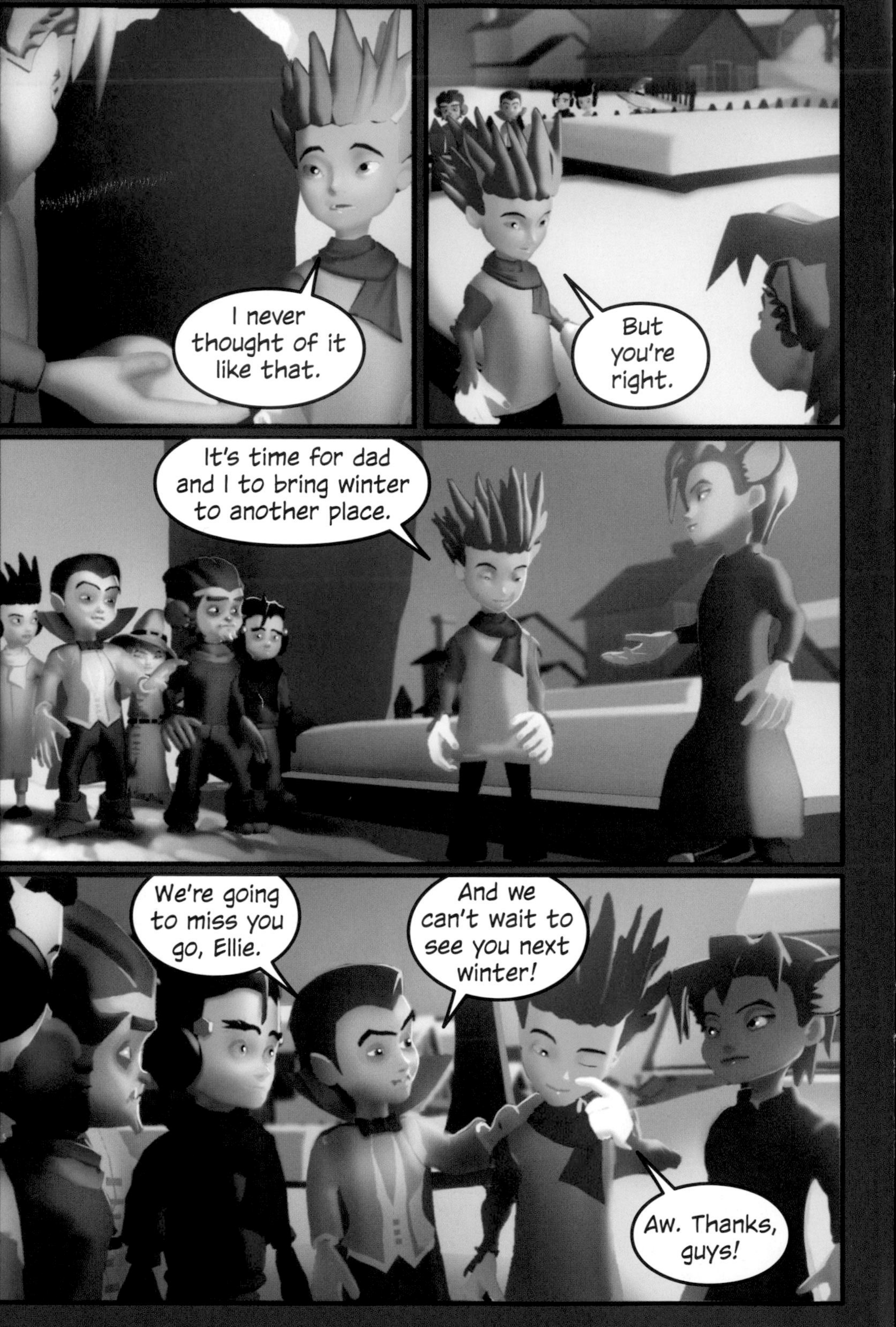
I never thought of it like that.
But you're right.
It's time for dad and I to bring winter to another place.
We're going to miss you go, Ellie.
And we can't wait to see you next winter!
Aw. Thanks, guys!

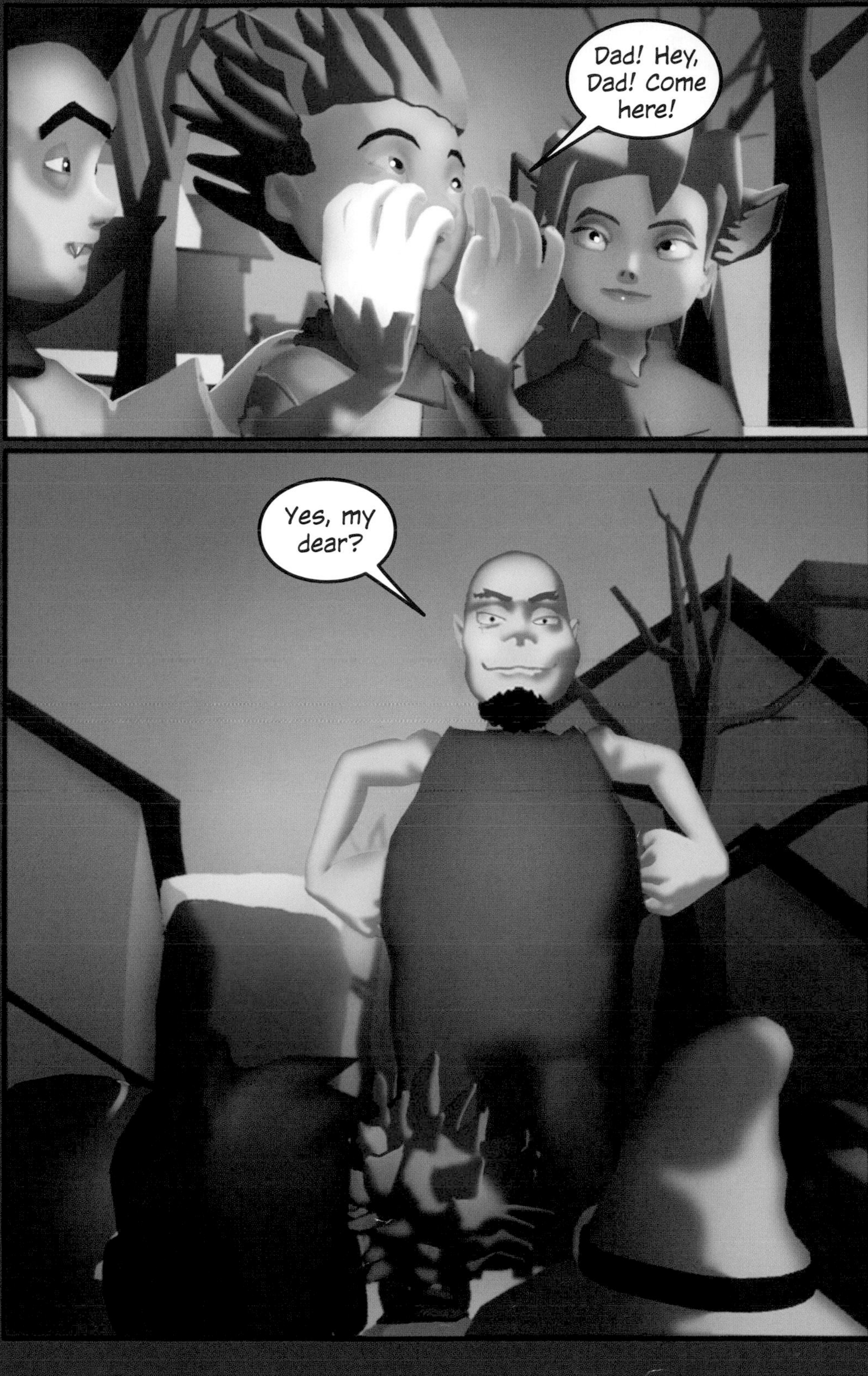
Dad! Hey, Dad! Come here!
Yes, my dear?

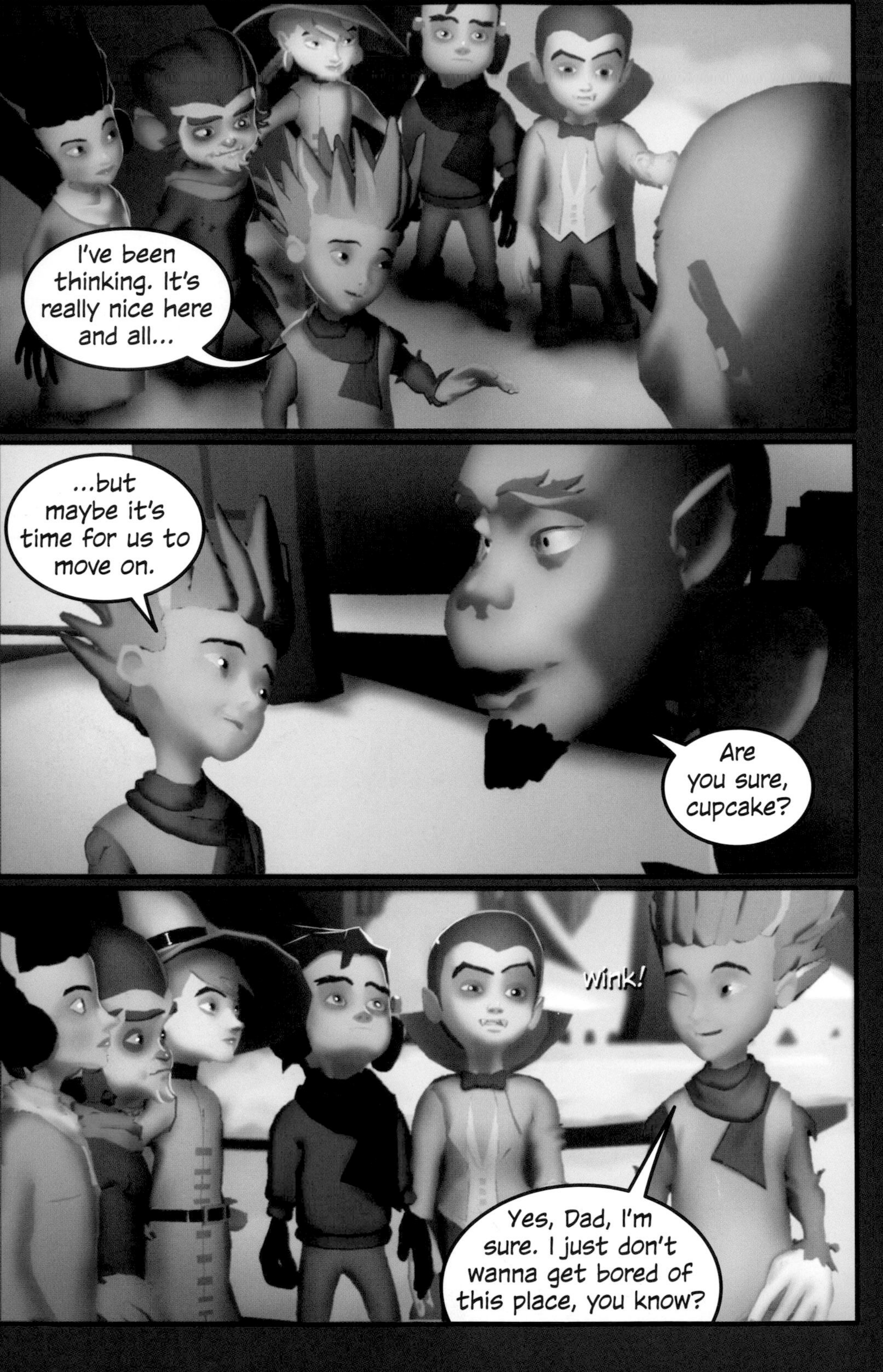
I've been thinking. It's really nice here and all...
...but maybe it's time for us to move on.
Are you sure, cupcake?
WINK!
Yes, Dad, I'm sure. I just don't wanna get bored of this place, you know?

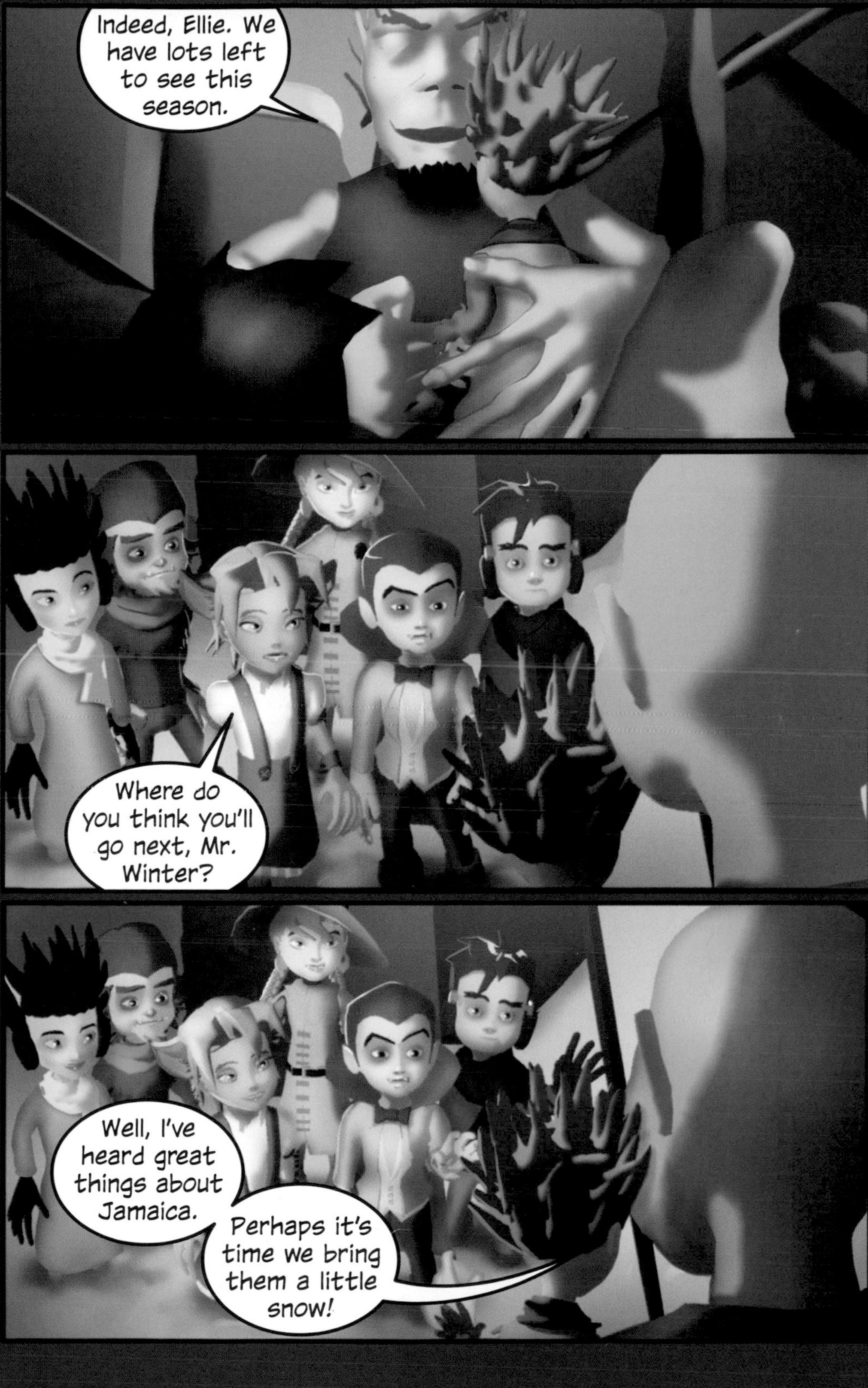
Indeed, Ellie. We have lots left to see this season.
Where do you think you'll go next, Mr. Winter?
Well, I've heard great things about Jamaica.
Perhaps it's time we bring them a little snow!

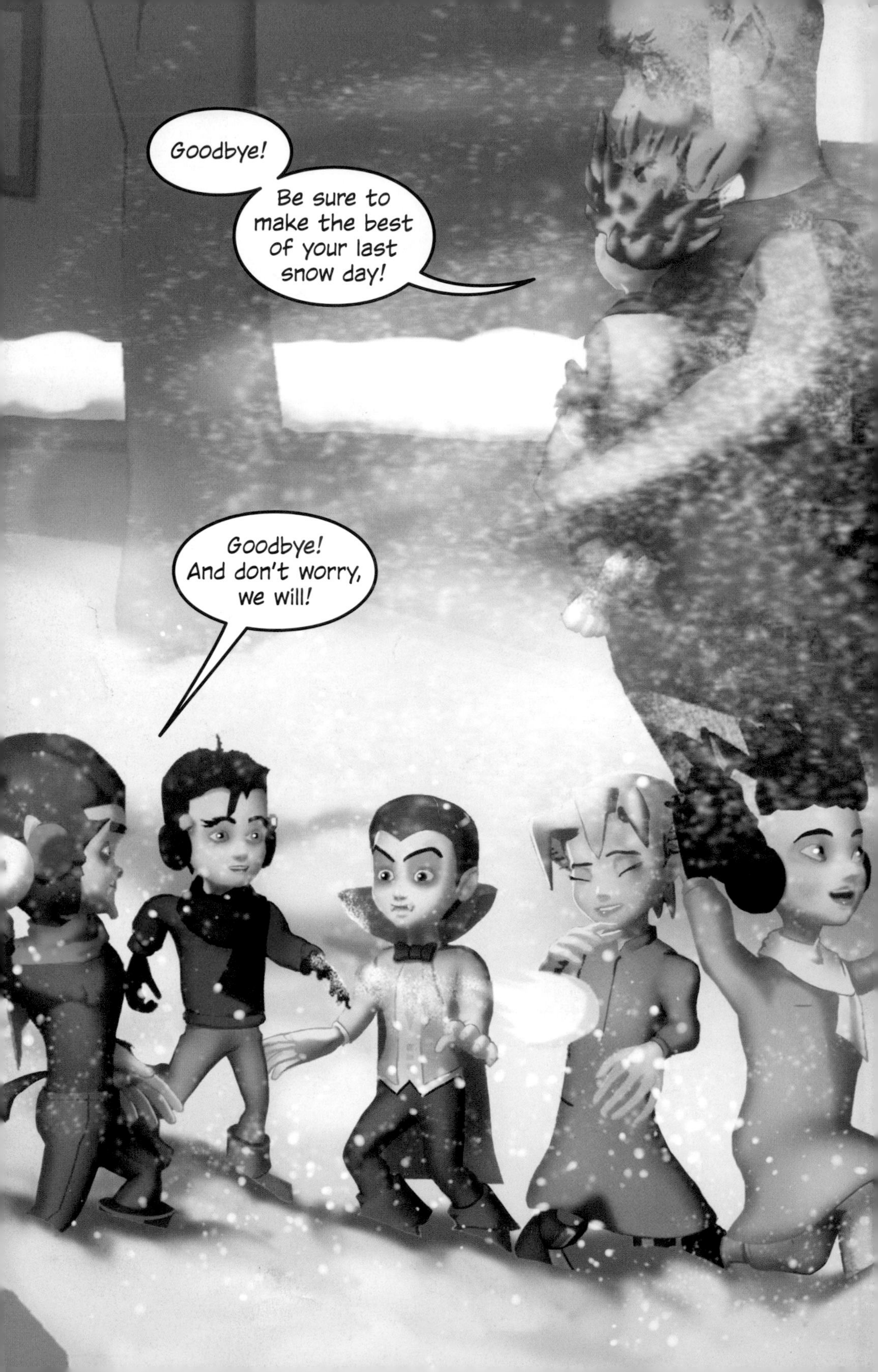
Goodbye!
Be sure to make the best of your last snow day!
Goodbye! And don't worry, we will!

Within a year, the company won many awards including the Shuster Award for Outstanding Publisher and the Moonbeam Award for top children's graphic novel. O'Reilly also won the Top 40 Under 40 award from the city of Vancouver and authored The Clockwork Girl for Top Graphic Novel at Book Expo America in 2009. Currently, O'Reilly is one of the most prolific independent comic book writers in Canada. While showing no signs of slowing down in comics, he now writes screenplays and adapts his creations for the big screen.

# GLOSSARY

**appropriate** (uh-PROH-pree-uht)–suitable for the situation, or right, as in appropriate attire

**blizzard** (BLIZ-urd)–a heavy snowstorm, often with strong winds

**climate** (KLYE-mit)–the usual weather in a certain place

**curious** (KYUR-ee-uhss)–eager to find something out, or interested in understanding how something works

**honest** (ON-ist)–an honest person is truthful who does not lie or steal or cheat

**officially** (uh-FISH-uhl-ee)–if something is official, it has been approved by someone in authority

**relax** (ri-LAKS)–to calm down, or become less tense and anxious

**tentacles** (TEN-tuh-kuhlz)–one of the long, flexible limbs of some animales like the octopus and squid

# DISCUSSION QUESTIONS

1. Which Mighty Mighty Monster is your favorite? Why? Discuss your favorite monsters.

2. As long as Ellie is in Transylmania, there will never be another spring. If you could have only one season for the rest of your life, which one would you choose? Why?

3. Old Man Winter can travel anywhere in the world instantly. If you could teleport, where would you go? What places would you visit? Talk about traveling.

# WRITING PROMPTS

1. Imagine another new monster has come to Transylmania. Who is he or she? Write about your new monster, and then draw a picture of him or her.

2. The Mighty Mighty Monsters get a snow day. What would you do if school were canceled because of a blizzard? Write about your day off.

3. Even though they're friends, the gang has to tell Ellie to leave. Have you ever told someone you cared about something that wasn't easy to say? Write about it.

# Mighty Mighty MONSTERS ADVENTURES

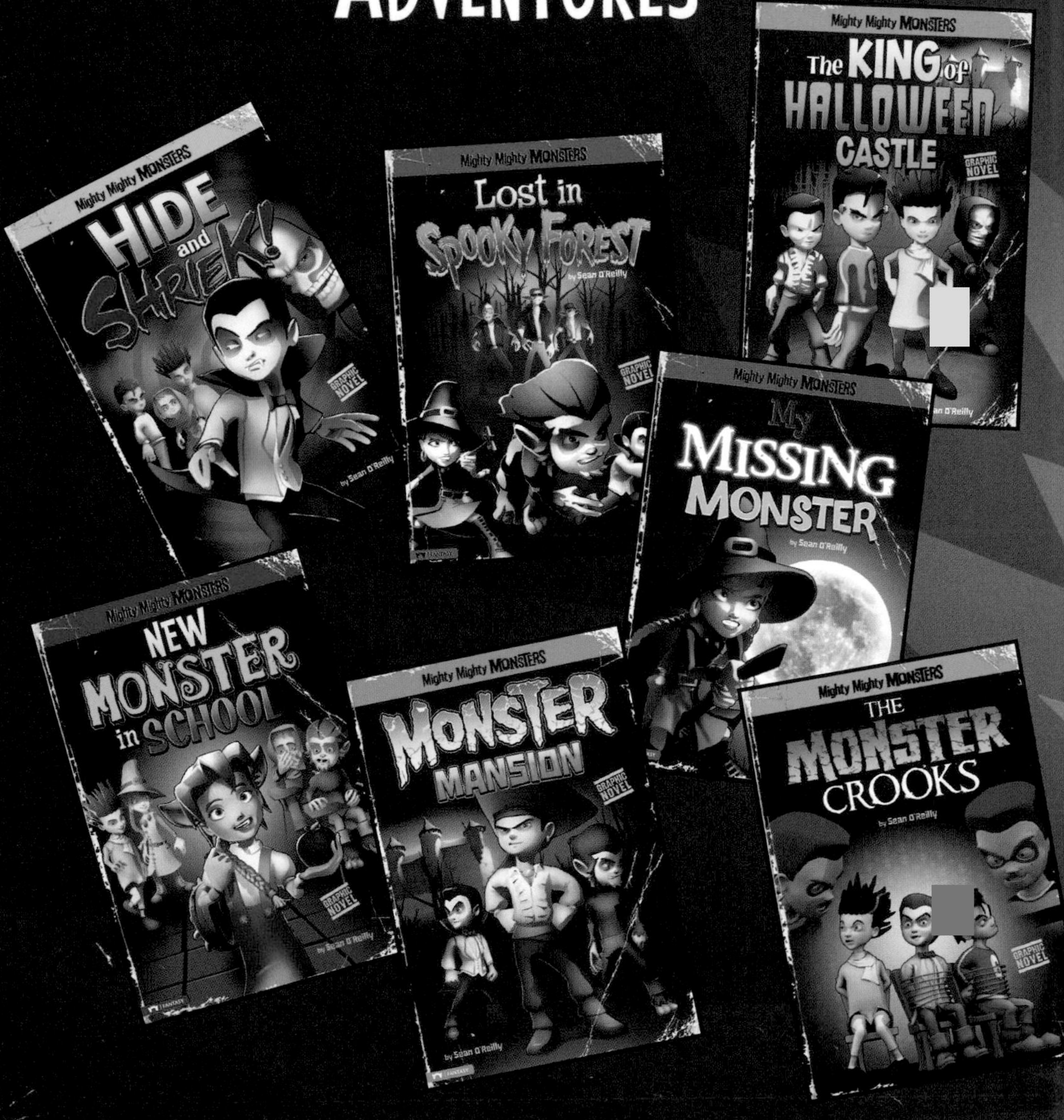
Mighty Mighty MONSTERS
HIDE and SHRIEK!
by Sean O'Reilly
GRAPHIC NOVEL
Mighty Mighty MONSTERS
Lost in Spooky Forest
by Sean O'Reilly
GRAPHIC NOVEL
Mighty Mighty MONSTERS
The KING of HALLOWEEN CASTLE
GRAPHIC NOVEL
Mighty Mighty MONSTERS
My MISSING MONSTER
by Sean O'Reilly
Mighty Mighty MONSTERS
NEW MONSTER in SCHOOL
GRAPHIC NOVEL
by Sean O'Reilly
Mighty Mighty MONSTERS
MONSTER MANSION
GRAPHIC NOVEL
by Sean O'Reilly
Mighty Mighty MONSTERS
THE MONSTER CROOKS
by Sean O'Reilly
GRAPHIC NOVEL

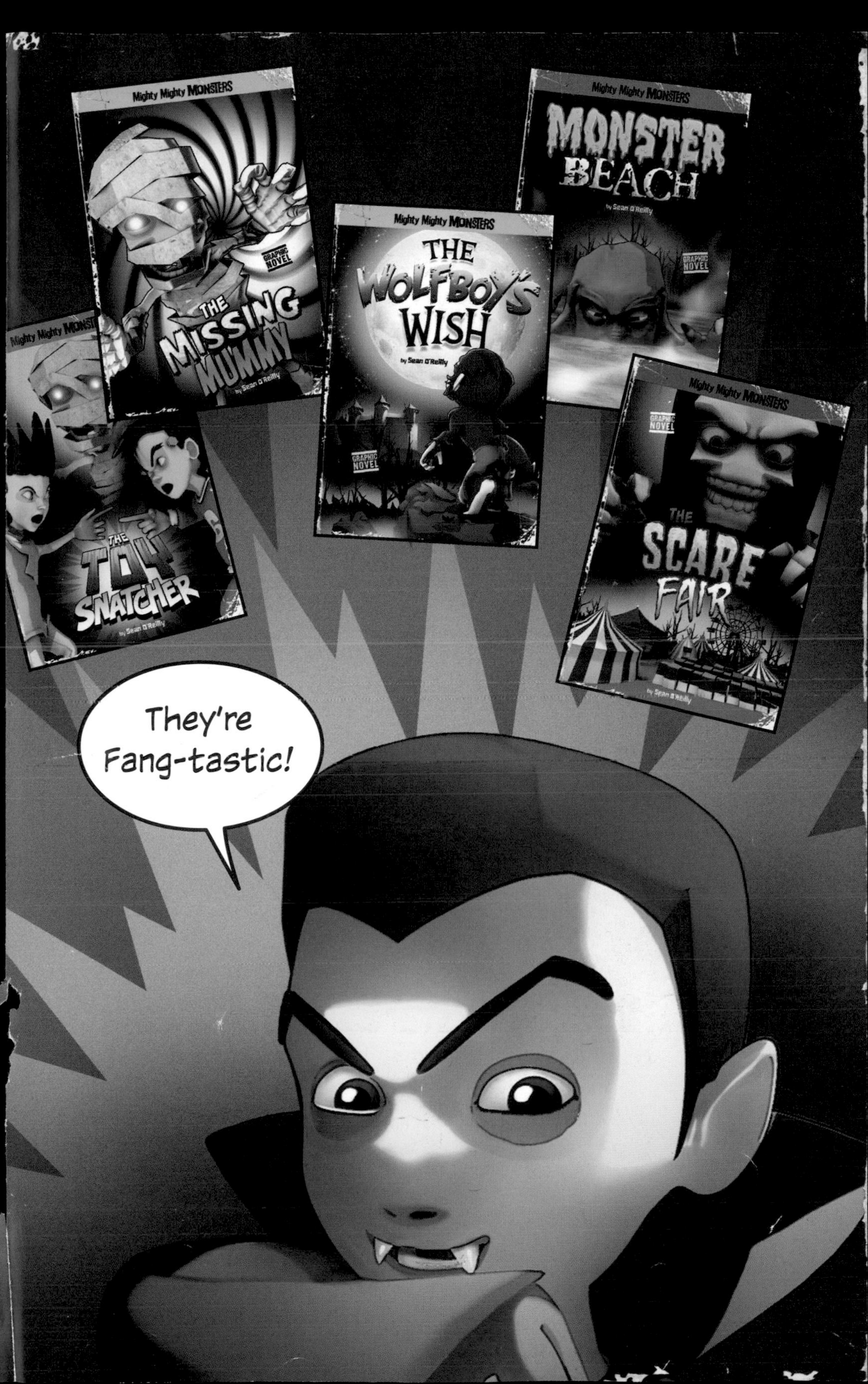
Mighty Mighty MONSTERS
THE MISSING MUMMY
GRAPHIC NOVEL
by Sean O'Reilly
Mighty Mighty MONSTERS
THE WOLFBOY'S WISH
by Sean O'Reilly
GRAPHIC NOVEL
Mighty Mighty MONSTERS
MONSTER BEACH
by Sean O'Reilly
GRAPHIC NOVEL
Mighty Mighty MONSTERS
THE TOY SNATCHER
by Sean O'Reilly
Mighty Mighty MONSTERS
GRAPHIC NOVEL
THE SCARE FAIR
by Sean O'Reilly
They're Fang-tastic!